I0678720

The Missing Link:
The Story of Charles

by

Adriane Kross

TELEMACHUS PRESS

If you purchased this book without a cover you should be aware that this book is stolen property. It was reported as "unsold and destroyed" to the publisher and neither the author nor the publisher has received any payment for this "stripped book."

This book is a work of fiction. Names, characters, places and incidents are either the product of the author's imagination or are used fictitiously. Any resemblance to actual persons, living or dead, or to actual events or locales is entirely coincidental.

The Missing Link: The Story of Charles
Copyright © 2012 Adriane Kross. All rights reserved, including the right to reproduce this book, or portions thereof, in any form. No part of this text may be reproduced, transmitted, downloaded, decompiled, reverse engineered, or stored in or introduced into any information storage and retrieval system, in any form or by any means, whether electronic or mechanical without the express written permission of the author. The scanning, uploading, and distribution of this book via the Internet or via any other means without the permission of the publisher is illegal and punishable by law. Please purchase only authorized electronic editions and do not participate in or encourage electronic piracy of copyrighted materials.

The publisher does not have any control over and does not assume any responsibility for author or third-party websites or their content.

Cover Designed by Telemachus Press, LLC

Cover Art:
Copyright © Thinkstock/86493780/Comstock
Copyright © Thinkstock/200284360-001/Photodisc

Published by Telemachus Press, LLC
http://www.telemachuspress.com

ISBN# 978-1-937698-80-5 (eBook)
ISBN# 978-1-937698-81-2 (paperback)

Version 2015.04.24

Printed in the United States of America

10 9 8 7 6 5 4 3 2 1

Dedication

The book is dedicated to all the people who Charles has affected in hopes that by reading this story you are never alone. For the social workers, this book is also dedicated, for when an individual is needing help, there should always be an in-depth investigation on the person who is being seen. And last for all the people who made this book possible, especially Sheila, the scientist in Washington, D.C., and Rebecca with her belief intelligence.

Dedication

The Missing Link:
The Story of Charles

Chapter 1

MARY COULD NOT stand to be near Charles after that small voice would not allow her to even keep thoughts of him in her mind. Charles's tears flowed as he walked away from Mary yet the sting of his rejection prompted his remarking, "You will be sorry for that!" He left with a bitter disdain upon all who he encountered thereafter.

Charles could not forget Mary after that one week of encounter. They talked and laughed. All was wonderful he thought in his mind until that day of rejection. His hatred for all women was unleashed. With the voice of sweetness, there was a slamming of the door by Mary's reverberating statement, "No, I do not want to be your friend." Even his mother could not console the hurt Charles felt. This was a blow to his control. For no one rejected Charles. Mary that inconsiderate being, "Why would you do this to me?"

Charles felt nothing for the battle of Ben. He did have a feeling of accomplishment. The kind of accomplishment that the headhunters have after shrinking the head and wearing it around their neck as a trophy. Poor Ben walked away in silence trying to figure out what went wrong and how things could have been different. Ben never wanted to battle over Mary, he just wanted Mary's energy for himself. That sweet smell of innocence that gave way to the goodness she stood for and truly was. Ben left with a sneer of regret and a promise to himself that he would be back when the time was right. However, that time was not now nor would it be for some time. The pain of defeat was greater than his winning, for this battle was between forces of the dark, and the defeat of Mary's light, the light that gave way to a brilliance that few had ever known. Charles that cunning fox, only battled to fight for control. Control of a being he thought was naïve and frail. Yet her light outshined his darkness and for this he bowed down to realms he knew nothing about. These light matters were taken up through higher orders of beings who constantly watched over Mary. Yet Charles pursued his path of resistence and wanted Mary to be of his light, the light of evil and backward motion on the spiraling chain of command.

His wheels continued churning inside reaching to the depth of his soul. Those imagined hurts were festering deep down every day and hour. These misguided wrongs had infringed on his tainted soul that left scars of hatred and revenge sometime or another. There were angers that rose from the depths of his heart to the heights of his madness. Yet Mary, in some odd way, was pressed into some small hole of reprieve that peeked out every once in awhile. She tenderized his heart, but only for a brief moment of less disheartened solace. The thought of Mary finding her true love was not only appalling to Charles, but ever present. Charles was always hoping that Mary would find the error of her ways and finally come home to him. In Charles mind, she belonged to him, and him only.

As he often thought about his revengeful plots, he discovered something about Mary and her beloved. A fiendish plot needed to be executed. As Charles looked to his Forefather's past he realized that he came into this life to settle a vendetta. In another lifetime, Mary's soul mate had taken away Charles's animals for payment of a debt. He loved his animals. He returned in this life for vengeance. This was a silly matter but to Charles this meant the world. For anything taken from him was cause enough for revenge in any lifetime. Charles could stand in front of you and see all your past lives and how they intertwined with him. He was a true master magician of deception.

Charles' most interesting past life with Mary was when they were both metaphysicians and both had their own power, yet Mary was always of a higher order than Charles and for this Charles became furious as it came to him. Charles also remembered a life with Mary in Atlantis and he had destroyed Mary and her soul mate then. The aperture of love would not fully blossom. It is in this lifetime that Charles would make sure that Mary would have a life full of yearning of what may be, an unfulfilled and restless existence. Charles was not only a remote viewer with a keen intelligence and microscopic view, he had Aspergers' Syndrome, he was above the norm.

At the time, Mary's soul mate was ending a relationship. Charles looked into this matter and decided to Use mind control on this other woman. He was able to manipulate and control her mind by degrading and demoralizing Mary's soul mate. This in turn brought a shocking ending to Mary's soul mate's romance that scarred him in a state of never wanting to be married or for that matter ever wanting to commit to anyone. Thank goodness Mary's soul mate was able to overcome this and move on in his life with Mary. Yet, unbeknownst to Mary, the realization never crossed her mind nor ever became present until the soul mate decided to divulge his true feelings about the woman. Mary never understood what had happened to her soul mate until a friend did a thorough healing on her and discovered this and told her. At that moment, Mary never knew the depth to which Charles could steep to.

There was another depth that even Mary could not fathom and that was from a friend of Charles's. Charles had many cronies, but this particular one got in touch with Mary. Charles asked his friend to render a service for which his friend had a peculiar specialty. That specialty consisted of sending energy to a sun spot that would touch Mary during a dream state. During this dream state, Mary would envision a trauma to one of her family members and thus place her in a vulnerable state of disappointment and hardship. Charles found happiness in being able to spread misery and misfortune to Mary, thus making her feel humble and not one of happiness or joy, but one of misfortune. During this feeling of misfortune, Charles could relate to Mary, for she was vulnerable and his overprotection and bullying made him take charge of all he thought was his. Why should Mary feel happiness and joy while searching for her soul mate, when he was feeling alone and sad? And besides, why should she choose him over Charles?

The ever persistent Charles also tried to send vibrational waves of negativity that left Mary with unwavering lack of confidence in all that she did. These waves of negativity were done at a high pitch that reverberated the walls of Mary's domain. Mary prayed for this to pass. He struck down all jobs that she sought with these waves that also left an alarming shroud of discontent. Poor Charles, the feeling of never being loved or never experiencing love, were removed and replaced with all the hatred and anger that churned like a fierce tornado that swept all the rubble and dirt in a swirling fury around him and with those around him too.

The ever threat of those who brought misery to Charles were placed on a list like Adriane Messenger, who were struck off with indelible ink, as injustices were done. This list consisted of people Adriane was going to murder in a movie mystery. Those ever faithful comrades were ever persistent with commands and onslaughts, that few took notice of what truly was going on. Those comrades never asked questions of why or what, but remained steadfast to their leader, especially since Charles kept this demon hidden and was brought out upon occasion when his cronies became troublesome or an adversary threatened him. His cronies feared his commands and few dared cross the line to disobey. If one disobeyed, one would have to fight Charles and the demon. Although few tried, there were a few who dared and lost in a mist of downward negative waves under the category of lost souls and distraught fools who dare even to try. Yet, under this mask of bullying and possessed soul, lay a blank slate of a child with blonde hair that found life to be full of stupid naïve people who could be duped by a creature like him and someone who could communicate with intelligence that was awed by some. For those who knew of him, he was sight to behold. For under the veneer was an evil of unprecedented Biblical proportion that was unleashed whenever the dark forces decided to do so. These dark forces were from a universe far away that found Charles to be a conduit due to his vulnerability at an early age and when he was diagnosed as having Asperger's Syndrome. There were twenty entities that gave way to twenty personalities. Charles mimicked these evil souls by following their evil commands while Charles mistook their evil ways for his own. Those evil doers found Charles at a young age and attached themselves throughout his life to execute their evil deeds.

Mary for quite some time thought Charles found these beings by accident, but that was not so. In this manner, one could look at Charles and perhaps imagine some hope that lay within his being. For maybe Charles was not responsible for his evil doing. However one never knew if Charles had beckoned their help or they worked through him.

He was possessed, and who but a possessed person would follow their commands. A child is naïve and would never suspect any evil being occupying their psyche, let alone their entire being. Or could his mother have been the culprit who summoned these beings to give her son his strength of a mythical God from beyond? Those ideas became more evident with Mary and never left her thoughts. In this respect, who would dare go against Charles? Ah, this was his mother's plan and one that would allow him to hide behind Asperger's Syndrome.

Diabolically, Charles's mother followed this plan and masked his innate negativity that hid a monster that no one could defeat. The ball and chain of his big demon only hid the true motive of his evil plots and precision work to go after his prey with much deep thought and angry compulsion. This large demon with burning red eyes was seen by Mary but she never moved while in his presence. And these evil creatures from a galaxy not near ours, had a foothold in Charles to bring chaos and disarray to all here on earth. Their plan from afar rested in their taking hold of earth not too far in the distant future.

Mary never detected such a plan, but found glimpses of strange movements and altered happenings when talking to Charles. Although Charles was a strange being, he never let on about these entities from afar. These beings never let Charles know all their powers. Charles would thus feel that he was partly responsible for all that he did or said and sometimes thought he was in control of all. These negative beings made contact with him when he least suspected and were heard on a high frequency during an episode when he was in combat with those that opposed him. The heightened velocity of darkness connected with the darkness of the outer universe. that disguising factor that leads others to believe that like-minded flock together, even if they are from other galaxies. The negative beings knew that Charles would follow their command and execute their plan to destroy or harm those who were of the light and did good deeds on this planet earth. Thus another reason why Charles targeted Mary and yet Charles would not destroy Mary, at least not now.

Charles, the bully, controlled by a mother who sought her own power found refuge with the help of these aliens. Yet, he never knew where their power began and his ended. Eventually he and they became as one. Charles's father could have helped avoid such things, but he died while Charles was six years old. The changing of the tide can always be turned, but this would have made it much easier from the beginning of life than later. The glowing love a father has for his son could have changed Charles, but the lost love that needed to be there, was masked by an evil soul, an ever present mother. She enacted her evil deeds behind the innocence of a boy who could have been different. We are all given the right to choose between light and those opposing that light and Charles was never given that opportunity at a young age. Mommy dearest saw to that!

We are able to rise above our own misgivings despite what we have around us. It is up to us to change to whomever we want to be. Charles was not able to rise above his mother and Charles went through much of his life being in a child-like state of mind that was similar to a boy dunking Mary's pigtails in ink. His dark thoughts and negative perspective led him to seek revenge for the tiniest insult or perceived injustice. Everything was a sinister joke that only he could do without anyone knowing and he kept that secret very well. Those who knew Charles dared to tell for silence would be forever felt. The joke of the century was with Charles and he felt a heroic self-righteousness that gave him the courage to execute those dastardly deeds. Those negative aliens who comforted and edged him onto believing he was all that he was!

Yet, Charles could not see that without these entities, this missing link was a shallow, fearful being that was controlled not only by these aliens, but a destructive mother who was selfish and very evil. Her evil mind led Charles to believe that she was his world forever, without questioning any thought to the other side of life, one of happiness, joy and love. Mary gave him that chance, but Charles was unable to acknowledge the love he so desperately needed. The love of friendship. That time had passed and in its place, Charles replaced it with anger and frustration on how anyone could do this to him and how Mary could pass him over for an intimate relationship. Mary continued to have compassion for Charles, but as these hateful and evil misgivings threatened her life and her love, her soul mate, Mary became angry and this fed the darkness of Charles even more.

Prayer was the only thing that gave Mary hope in a never-ending situation that Charles would not let up nor relinquish. Forgiveness was forever on Mary's lips that she kept repeating with a relentless persistence that gave way to an unorthodox binding that Charles enacted. For when she was in trouble, Mary found that the Supreme Being wanted her to be closer to him, and in this way, Mary knew Charles had a purpose in her life. The kindness of Mary led Charles on an ever persistence of her soul that bound her fears and manipulated her soul and spirit. Are those things possible? Charles, who studied such things when left alone in the presence of his mother, found that this was the only way he could keep Mary close to him. Mary found Charles as a test to her faith. And Charles found her a challenge to his way of life.

To overcome Charles, Mary had to fight senseless battles, resort to craftiness, and keep ever vigilant for underhanded throws of mud that Charles kept slinging. Having no down time, Charles's cronies assisted Charles to win his power over hers. Charles thwarted all who got too close to Mary and used mind control on others around her to spy or keep Mary in line. Mary would use her intuition instead of her head, and that kept her grounded and ever vigilant with Charles's every move. Tied to victory was an event that would barely keep Mary alive, yet she remained unscathed and without fear of what she was about to encounter. Mary never felt paralyzed by Charles, she thought he was a jokester who needed to be reckoned with.

Looking back at Charles, Mary found that deceit and plotting was very great in Charles. The game of life that he lived was much more than feeling he was a Supreme God. Should one feel sorry that he was possessed or that he was a lost soul with a mother who plotted his course? We all are given that choice of who we pay allegiance to and Charles was no different. He made this choice long ago under the influence of mommy dearest, but he was able to make that choice with his own intelligence and his own being. The others, his cronies, were flittering flickers of darkness that came to attention when the voice of Charles rang them to order. The demon behind Charles was just an added prop to bring them to that order, lest they stray or decide to disobey the shepherd's command. The motley crews of undesirables were a strange crew, yet these misfits always obeyed without any complaints and without any disagreements. Their hero Charles who showed them tricks and reveled in their faithfulness willingly.

Sometimes they were older comrades or young ones, who Charles felt he could help, mold and shape. Charles would promise wealth and riches for their control of others. Their ignorant beliefs led them down a road of hardship and bewilderment when Charles left them without a trace. Yet those who knew Charles stood back and watched how Charles, the odd character that he was, worked his wonders and moved with the grace of an elephant and the destruction of a wild tornado. He was the creeper who slimed through society and performed as though he were a magician and sorcerer of great intelligence. That imposter! For who would bother to care about such foolish and degrading acts of moral and unethical degradation of the human being and soul. Charles was the answer to life's abomination of all those who went astray and found refuge in all that was not wholesome and not of love. He could never reach the heights of love to the Supreme Being, and thus fell to the ever depths of hatred and revenge. We all have a shadow side and Charles was possessed with relentless spirits who vibrated at low negative vibrations and walked with him in a spirit of disturbing falsehoods.

Mary forgave him after that week of friendship, despite the injustices he performed on her, as the Supreme Being had forgiven her and all others. Mary came to know herself better by finding that Charles reflected in her, all negative aspects of herself that she never reflected on nor would ever want to again. We so often look at only one side of ourselves and never relinquish the other. For this, Mary was grateful to Charles, and tried to understand the depth of her being and soul.

As for Mary's soul mate, this contract of a past life needed to be mended. Charles came into this life with the understanding that he would seek vengeance when meeting Mary's soul mate. The question of intelligence or ignorance is one to be pondered on, for do we release all that has happened with an act of atonement or do we seek vengeance for things of the past? No matter how intelligent Charles had been, his downward spiraling never allowed him to reach the heights that Mary had attained.

As Charles's cronies came to his beck and call, Mary knew friends and helpers who also watched over her and gave her advice. Kathleen, Chris and Linda continued to be there when Mary felt her privacy violated or acts of whirlwind anger were felt through the winding down of her spirit. Their consoling healing words comforted her lonely, distraught and frightened glimpses of how negativity invaded her being. She was told that her strength and her faith were related to an energy of the beyond and a being at the time of her birth had always accompanied her throughout her life. Mary was able to see her life in another manner after this and found that she was never alone, even when great trials with Charles or Ben frightened her to the very core. The more afraid Mary had been, the easier it was for Charles to enter Mary's energy and control her. Ben that staturesque figure of a man, who resembled Mark Twain, went to battle with Charles and lost. For Charles started a battle with Ben and was the victor.

Charles strived to win for the sake of being a heroic figure in the eyes of Mary.

Mary found nature to be comforting and healing whenever Charles attacked or his cronies brought a lingering vibration of confusion and disarray. Mary kept in much contact with Kathleen, Chris and Linda, but as Mary grew in spirituality, a new set of friends were escorted in. However Kathleen, Chris and Linda were instrumental and consulted for they knew Mary very well! Their consistent light burned brightly in the heart of Mary.

It is similar to our guides. When we have outgrown our guides we usually loose one or two and are replaced. They have done their work and now it is time to bring in greater guides who present a greater challenge to Mary and her facing greater challenges, she needed guides who could meet those challenges. So it was with her circle of healers and friends.

Chapter 2

DOWN THE ROAD of eternal faith, Mary met a man named Jeremy, an older gentleman, who stated that we are all Gods. The disdain of his words came forth a righteousness of indignation and arrogance. Jeremy was a man who was a leader of like souls yet when danger arose or negative forces became strong their door of "Like Godliness," was shut with a firmness to remind others of their ignorance and depth of a shallow pond.

"Oh, call day or night," he said.

Mary found some hope, but in a few days he stated he would consult with others to reach a solution. To Mary's surprise, he spoke to her in a message. "Each day is anew and look at it as such. Now I have done all I could, God bless you." To Mary's dismay he never answered his phone again, only a recording to his self righteous voice, "just call anytime." A pompous epitome of stately manner that found refuge with those of like camaraderie, who stood behind a dying breed. No need for Mary to look down this road, for the door to fight Charles was her battle alone without Jeremy, and that Charles made certain. If any soul reached the door of this older gentleman, they would find behind door number two the voice of a man of lost hope with a shocking slap of disbelief and a shaking of what went wrong. No need to go knocking here, no, Mary just keep walking.

Jason was the next man who Mary encountered. Mary did not go looking for him. He was a man that the Supreme Being sent. He was a godly soul that spoke of only godly things. He was a prophet of old who many came to hear and ask questions from. His meeting was one to remember, for his kind nature and his angelic ways led others to follow without any coercion. Mary met him while walking on her daily road into nature. He sent demons running and called to the Holy Ghost for Mary. All was gone and only the bright light remained. Jason spoke of his self as only a godly messenger, as godly people rarely speak otherwise. He helped Mary to remember that a greater power is steering her path and to remember this for all time. Did Mary forget her faith? Jason brought her back to this realization and her truth. His seat is reserved to all those that are holy in the hereafter, already in reserve and already taken.

As time passed and Mary was searching for her soul mate Mary realized that Charles was very devious to the point that she needed to know his next move. Charles wanted to control Mary. The evil who controlled Charles wanted to put out the light, that freedom with restriction and obedience. Being ahead of Charles's steps made his defeat possible. This was not a game of win or loose, evil against light, this was all about freedom. To be yourself and to live the life you choose is everyone's right. And any victory over Charles brought an opening to freedom.

A woman who was attuned to Mary's concerns knew of a man named Charlemagne. Charlemagne was a stately fellow that possessed an air of arrogance with the romantic mystique of someone who resembled an Italian actor, Rudolph Valentino of the 1920's.

He was very handsome and knew just what to say and when. Charlemagne at once knew that Mary was in a frenzied state due to all these attacks coming from Charles and he tried his best to help her with expediency and dedication. He told Mary, "Charles had mimicked another life-time of the 1900's when he had been rejected by you. You and Charles were both doctors, metaphysicians, and were of a high order. It is then that Charles resented the powers of you. He then tried to control you as he had in this life time."

Charlemagne told Mary that Charles brought forth his various personalities that resonated to the realm of that past life and became the man of that time. So many portals needed to be closed so that no more energy could be taken from Mary and all that she knew. The voice of yesterday rang to the theme of today with a loud reminiscent vibration. Mary quickly asked Charlemagne to help and he did. Mary was forever grateful the Charlemagne understood her and together they were able to piece together the connection between Charles and Mary. Mary thought Charlemagne would be always in her life but Mary would never see him again. He moved somewhere in Europe doing his work and helping others like Mary. He once sent her a note that stated,

"Thinking of you," that Mary kept pressed in her book of friends.

Although Charles and Mary had six past lives together, Mary also had to distinguish all past lives with her soul mate and Charles. In this way, nothing would be left unturned. Charlemagne had an associate that he would call from time to time to consult. His name was Peter. While Charlemagne was away, Peter would help Mary. Peter was also called in to add anything that was left out by Charlemagne, but his fear of Charles lashing out at him was too great and he would be as brief as possible when asked anything about a past life with Charles. Charles would know when any past life was being tampered with and this alerted him as to a door being shut to Mary. All of Charles's markers were in place and far be it Peter to disturb any of them. Mary understood Peter's apprehension and waited when both he and Charlemagne could help together. Peter was a past life regressionist that knew his trade well. But he also cherished his freedom and would not cross any line where Charles was concerned.

To this day, Mary had been in the battle with Charles for four and a half years and Mary reached for anything to end this senseless battle that was forever relentless, day and night, hour and minute to the hands of a madman. Mary was tired and that was what Charles had hoped for.

"Give in to me," he whispered. "You will never win." But she never paid attention to those voices. Who knew that those voices were only from Charles?

After so much time passing with this battle with Charles, Mary began to recap all that had been done to her. Doing so, she could recall and go back to the time she had just met

Charles and maybe, she would be able to find the source of why this happened. By cutting the problem at its source, she would end this battle. If Mary had her fears bound and her soul and spirit manipulated, she needed to find someone who could undo this. Charles's cronies would beat down Mary into submission, using confusion, blocking and taking her energy at will. Then the hatchet man would enter the picture and upon request of Charles, would wind down Mary's strong drive, giving way to inertia and depression. The hatchet man was a man who had a particular specialty. He would reach your higher self and then work from this position. These cronies as well as the other cronies of Charles, felt important when in the presence of Charles. It is at that precise moment that their expertise was called upon to demonstrate their anger of their world and their cruelty upon others. They were given that chance to prove their powers.

Charles's role of bullying and submission were played quite well by him. But who really knew the real Charles? Without his props or cronies, there was a petty tyrant that chose to build up these appearances and make himself what he longed to be. He wanted to be a real person who was loved and needed. He wanted to have a family who cared and listened. However, Mommy never gave him that chance. That despicable soul!

Sadness from time to time would overtake Mary when Charles would bother her soul mate and cause such negative thoughts and negative energies to encircle him. For Mary's soul mate knew nothing of Charles and would wonder about his own fate and how the Supreme Being had been unkind to him. Who was there to tell him otherwise? Mary was not there to guide him and relieve his conscious of any guilt of his perceived ways. The soul mate's mother once entered Mary's dream in order to tell her that her son needed her help. Mary then saw him walking to and fro, like Frankenstein. All Mary could do was weep and cry, for she needed to reach out, but only the Supreme Being heard her. Mary prayed for him to keep him safe and unharmed.

Mary also saw that her friends were being manipulated by Charles and at any time Mary would be close to meeting her soul mate, each friend would inadvertently call her to pull her away with something or other. Mary knew these games very well. One important news was from the shaman, Kathleen. Mary trusted her, but unbeknownst to Mary, Kathleen was also waiting on an inheritance. She also had a spell put on her by a witch, to never meet her soul mate. As she was combating Charles one day, the dark energies had gotten to her, her mind and soul changed to the dark side. The seed of discontent in Kathleen gave rise to a new Kathleen. This Kathleen was angry over her discontented life and the injustices that had been done to her. She let the door open to Charles and could then never close it. She could not thwart the darkness that Charles flung at her and thus her light was distinguished, as a burning coal that turned to ash.

Mary then discovered that Kathleen had stepped into Mary's life and manipulated her life for the life she too was meant to have, but lived it through Mary. The dark seed already implanted in Kathleen took on a different light and from then on, Kathleen became an enemy of hers. Mr. Hyde eventually took over Dr. Jekyll. Now Charles and Kathleen were one. They telepathically knew each other's thoughts.

Mary knew that her freedom to meet her soul mate would be difficult, especially with this combined force.

The force of Charles took over Kathleen. But Kathleen had the choice also. Charles telepathically communicated with Kathleen and thus they were able to work together.

The jamming of the succession of events was not only an everyday occurrence, it was anticipated, and thus Mary knew that although she wished and planned for things to happen as such, they never did. Every day, at least three times a day, Charles kept a vigil watch to see that all that he had orchestrated was not moved or touched. Those chess pieces were never put into check mate; they were just moved for the game.

Charles thus directed the energy of Temptation at Mary for the sole purpose to keep her occupied, away from her soul mate. If we indulge in our temptations, we lose our view on our objective. Mary's temptation was food however, and her delight was in eating. This kept Mary contented. Her search for her soul mate led to the comfort of food itself.

Needless to say, she gained weight while looking for her soul mate. And the hundred demons Charles threw at Mary? A strategic fear tactic to keep Mary under his control. Mary, the brave heroine, fought them off and overcame her fear. She was fighting for her soul mate and all that she loved.

She was also fighting for her life.

Chapter 3

MARY WOULD NEVER allow Charles to have the upper hand. All her life was that of independence, joy, laughter and some tears. Only the Supreme Being had that right to change her life, no, not even Charles or for that matter Ben. Mary had to break free of these negative beings and her light would shine as before. The dark overshadowed her but not for long. She had to find a way to break through what Charles had created around her and to her. Thus the shattered pieces of glass that Charles had broken were being put back together, piece by piece. Mary then studied and tried to undo all that Charles would send energetically on a daily basis.

Mary lay down on her bed and began to recall how this all began. That small voice within her let her know that something odd about Charles was present. He so diligently tried to suffocate and blot out Mary, that Mary found it difficult to remember all that initially took place within that one week. The jigsaw puzzle of life that Mary had to piece together was a riddle that needed to be solved. Mary knew at this time there was a bigger picture, one that would give her a greater understanding of why this was happening. Maybe there were multiple reasons or just one, Mary just needed to know why this was happening to her. She never knew at the beginning about any alien encounters.

As Mary began to remember all about Charles, a sudden dream-like state gave rise to a long deep remembrance and Mary began to recall how she came to know Charles and what he was like before the battle commenced. If only Mary had listened to that small voice. Prior to her coming into this world, Mary had agreed to this path or assignment, we all do. Yet after that week of meeting Charles, she had wished that this assignment be given back or changed. And fear overcame her.

The price of freedom had come at a grave price, one that Mary never imagined. There comes a time in a person's life that one comes to a road of knowledge and a knowing of what might ensue. Of this road, Mary dared not speak of nor begin to ever fathom. Warriors may take this assignment, but not the fainthearted nor the powerfully empowered. Yet, on some subconscious level, Mary took the challenge and unknowingly went into this play not as a cameo appearance, but as the main character.

Lay fear aside, because this poindexter was able to see your fears and approach you carefully with the expertise of a tight fine wire. In his mind there was no one who he couldn't have control over. There was no one he couldn't make fearful and belittle. By pitting your fears against you, your vulnerability lay open, and Charles could take you off your path of life for a brief time or one of long duration. Beware if an Incubus or Succubus were sent. Mary was told that silk red underwear can be used. Humorous as it may be, it was true! What had led Mary to this current point, was the vulnerability of a former friend or lover, who through a relationship gone sour, he tried energetically to hinder Mary's life as much as possible. Ben was a writer and an artist who opened a door in Mary that should not have been opened. A past life lover who led Mary astray and down a crooked path. This was the story of Ben.

One day, Mary was introduced to a man through an old friend. A man appeared to her as rather strange, yet very intelligent. His name was Charles. He was no ordinary man, for he kept many secrets to himself. He was tall in stature and wore thick glasses. He could appear feminine and then at other times be similar to Andy Warhol. Mary's friend wanted to rid herself of Charles and decided that Mary would be a good candidate for her friend's final exit with no forwarding address. May this false friend find life a bitter sweet taste of skunk perfume and bitters.

He said, "I am a Healer and I can help you."

For a moment Mary thought he was pleasant, but then in the second moment the inner voice spoke to Mary with grave hesitation. Vulnerable Mary believed Charles and unfortunately did not listen to that small voice that told her to go inside and leave Charles alone. Mary felt sorry for

Charles's strange shy behavior. As they talked, he wanted to help with her problem that Mary had with Ben. Mary explained that Ben was an energetic consumer. All went well until Charles telepathically connected to Ben and went to battle. Charles wanted to prove he was a heroine who rescued Mary in distress and he wanted to win. Yet this victor had many strings attached. His quick thinking made him realize that creating this battle would give him reign over Mary. And Mary had no choice to concede after the battle had began. She had known prayer as her only battle against any foe.

The main character here was Charles's mother, who at a young age, abused him and taught him many things of the dark side. You see, she was a witch.

This witch thought only of herself and used Charles for her bidding. Unfortunately, Charles needed counseling when his father died. Instead, he buried his feelings with resentment and hatred. These feelings never went away, he began to develop a hatred for all women and their power.

Charles was also a powerful being, despite his mother's influence. Charles could see not only as a remote viewer, he could also telepathically and psychically reach you and your thoughts and become a blend of one. He would reach the very crevice of your soul and change it, dip it in negativity and proceed as though you were a creature under a microscope.

Charles had helped Mary with Ben, but back home after that first week encounter, he began to regard Mary as a butterfly stretched out on clips. He then divided the top and bottom of the body, poking holes into qigong points. By removing the guards to these points in the body, he was able to energetically enter without any problem.

He started these antics as a child with others and proceeded as an adult to perfect his technique. Charles would hinder others without their knowledge all his life. Mary was the person to try and stop this when she was attacked. Mary was not sure if others tried, but she was not going to let anyone take from her who she really was. Thank God, Mary was a stubborn child.

As first, Mary imagined that Charles was jealous of what was in store for her, of what could be in the future with her life but he was really all about control and possible a touch of love. He wanted control of Mary, control of Mary's world, and control of what he couldn't have or understand. He was a bully and thought his life was far superior to anyone. He was an intellect that matched Mary's but his life was that of seclusion with books and found refuge with evil knowledge about control and what it could bring to others.

Although highly intellectual, he had played these games not only on Mary, but also on others all his life. These games began as a child, when he told his mother that all he could see were monsters. They too roamed the world, trying to find souls to attack. He was thus trained from his youth to move energy and objects. He could reverse a person's fate so events would never turn out as you expected.

His mother trained him in the dark arts while his father, an unsuspecting soul, knew nothing of the matter. His mother only allowed him to move under her influence. Charles made certain that any goodness that was to come to any of his victims never arrived. Out of jealousy, he felt if he was not happy, then no one else should be. As he grew older, many were afraid to talk to him, for fear that he might change their life permanently without remorse. The striking similarity between a Twilight Zone episode of a young boy turning people into objects and sending them into the cornfield struck Mary with a familiarity that she could not ignore.

Charles wore many hats to seek out his latest victim. His main disguise was a healer. He would send out his scouts to find his victim and then the scout would introduce the two. Once the introduction took place, Charles would energetically take something and work from his findings.

The battle with Ben lasted one week. Mary thought there was something odd about his actions and his appearance. She decided to gently state that she thought it was not to their best interests to continue their friendship. To Mary's dismay, Charles responded, "I can mow down trees miles in length with my voice." And then his voice reached a high pitch to demonstrate all he could do. Mary then covered her ears.

He then proceeded to walk with a glare that could penetrate the walls of titanium steel.

Thereafter Charles would cry on the phone to appear as if he were sad of the departure. After a while, he became quite believable. Mary even thought that this just maybe was quite genuine and just maybe this was a cry for loneliness felt. That cry reminded her of when a child is smitten by other children, while they are playing.

"No one wants to be around me, and I have few friends," he remarked. Little did Mary know that he tortured all his friends and all became friend or foe in a matter of seconds.

"I happen to be very busy and I also have very few friends at this time," Mary said, listening to her small voice while Charles's cries were heard.

His mother called days later to ask Mary how she could have done this to Charles. The thought of a mother calling about her grown son was thoroughly absurd. Mary hung up the phone with much dismay and pretended that it didn't happen.

Under no circumstances would Mary see Charles again, or so she thought. Strange occurrences happened as the weeks went by. For instance, Mary's friends heard a whispering voice say to them to kill themselves. In a dream state, he would pose as familiar people you knew, but then would try to do strange things in the dream state. Then as time went on, energy was taken from them and nervousness replaced peacefulness and joy. His deep seated anger fed off of anger with resentment and ridicule. Curses, spells and occasional voodoo dolls with your name on them were given proper attention. Mary found one of these dolls near her car and wondered what it was. It was explained to her by a Jamaican friend to beware. Mary never became fearful, she just listened.

Mary wondered for quite some time what her part was in all of this. Was it karma or trusting the wrong person for help? She knew that her freedom needed to be found, and that is what she only knew to be of truth.

After much consternation, this missing link stayed like glue to Mary's every move. Charles would wave his hands, to the devil, Mary thought, and change your fate. Life was never how you expected nor wished it to be. He even had bad

Kaunas to take your wish with a blink of an eye. This Charles studied in great length. One thing was certain, Charles would vanquish and obliterate your wishes as though there were being sucked through a black hole, never to appear. Mary prayed for this not to happen.

This dark lord masqueraded as a confused soul with Asperger's Syndrome. Behind the curtain laid a heavy hand with repercussions beyond the Outer Limits. What a piece of work! Did the Supreme Being make this creature also? Mary hoped to think that under all the possession and myriad swamp of green ooze there was some hope.

Yet, Mary blamed his mother also, Charles's identical female version. A deadly spider that would use anyone to feed her own lack of power.

After much consternation and stirring of resentment, Charles began to show signs of indignation and anger. One night the outside doorknob started to move.

Since Charles could not enter any doorway, he began to stalk Mary. Stalking happened very often near Mary's house and also visiting her home with different cars outside her bedroom window. Mary decided to take him to court. The day of the trial, there outside the courtroom was his mother. An identical shadow who kept the strings of the puppet close to her heart. Mary's accused entered the courtroom with much bewilderment. Mary dared not look his way. There were not going to be any male or female medusas changing Mary to stone. Charles also kept the head of medusa around his neck for his own protection.

The whole time he fixed his attention toward the judge with all his power and might, controlling anything that he might infringe on him or incarcerate. There was an assistant at that time who sat with Mary for support. She was very comforting and consoling. Mary's knees were beginning to rattle. The work of Charles was trying to take hold.

As Mary stood up, all eyes were upon her. "In this courtroom your honor, the prisoners who wear chains are not to be feared, but this thing sitting to my right is worse than Jeffrey Dahmer, who killed his prey out in the open.

"This monster not only psychologically, but knowingly, attacks his victim and hides behind Asperger's Syndrome, the curtain of self-defense without a whimper. As he alters your life and you think God has been unkind to you or your luck has suddenly changed for the worse, you may never be the same after just speaking to this thing."

"It is my opinion, your honor, to have Charles sent to a state hospital, be under medication and be observed. It will be only then that you will see what he is capable of. Otherwise, if you allow this thing to be set free today, not only will I have to take cover and my family, but also you will have unleashed an evil that is uncontrollable on humanity, not to speak of the children and others he has affected."

At the time Mary felt she was speaking for all those he had touched who were crying for justice. She also felt the rage building in Charles and his trying so desperately to have Mary sit down and be silenced for good.

God surely was with Mary that day, even though the later verdict was not just.

The honorable judge had his mind controlled and decided to let Charles go since there was no visible evidence. Only Mary's hearsay and the fact that the phone company showed his phone number on Mary's bill. There were many times Charles came by Mary's house with different colored cars and would be gone. Yet, the honorable judge looked only at Mary as he passed down the sentence.

Mommy dearest stood outside, waiting for her darling to arrive with open arms. "We have won," he whispered to her, as they shuffled to the stairs.

As he arrived home, he received sympathy from other family members who felt these accusations were unjust and cruel. Dear Charles had been taken advantage of and falsely accused due to his misunderstood condition. At times of duress and adverse accusations, this comforted his lying conscious and his deceiving nature. Meanwhile his lies were almost believable to him, at least for little while.

To Mary's amazement, after she initially filled out the Police report on Charles, she found out that three other women had made a complaint, but never signed their names. Poor souls, Mary dared not think what they may have encountered!

Mary called on all of the light, including Masters, Angels and Guides who would be of service from the other side. At times she wondered if they were listening. Holy water, churches and sage were always in abundance and attended. Every morsel of her body was pitted on how truly faithful she had been or presently could be. Mary began to find ways to fight back against Charles. For this, Mary's faith was surely tested.

Chapter 4

OTHERS HELPED WITH their advice and the advice of others was discarded, Shamans presented themselves with very useful advice. However, a Shaman in California and a Shaman in Africa decided to get together and throw this demon named Charles into a lake of fire. His soul unwillingly went. However, after a few days, Charles's hand reached down to the abyss and resurfaced with the dark emanating.

To the Shamans' surprise they quickly refunded any monies given and bowed out gracefully. Mary investigated all Avenues to help combat against Charles. These avenues consisted of others who might know of such things. Mary's hope to her predicament was given light by others who tried to assist. Mary was open to all and allowed the Shamans to perfom their services. Their service of combating darkness.

Then a man Mary had met talked about lazering those not of the light. He had heard about what Mary was going through from a friend. He stepped forward and said, "Nothing ever exists after lazering." Twice Charles was lazered and twice he survived. This man kept saying that he did all he could and could not understand how it was possible?

There were others who, together with other healers, tried to disempower Charles, but all succumbed to the inevitable fate of discouragement and defeat. Charles had made calculated moves to go after his prey with a great deal of accuracy; that one would have to be psychic, telepathic and clairvoyant to anticipate his next move.

In these attempts to strip Charles of his powers, there was another important point that had to be re-considered. That point was a large demon he carried with him, who was brought out if need be. Charles also had twenty personalities. And these personalities gave rise to twenty entities that were not visible to the naked eye. The aliens kept him close and they kept a watchful eye on his every move.

Charles brought forward each entity whenever it suited him. His power came from a universe far away and those beings used Charles as a vehicle to create chaos and disruption among the godly creatures of this world. Charles was well aware of this at times.

With everyone we meet, we have chosen and have known before in other life times. For some reason, we act out the past play for one reason or another. We chose this lifetime to learn lessons and then move on or learn them again. We then aspire to higher realms if all is learned. However, other friends of Mary's suggested that she was at a place at the wrong time and there was no karmic reason. This was just a case of bad luck.

There was no rationalizing meeting Charles, for the strength of disturbed people has the strength of ten people without the addition of twenty personalities. The continual pursuit of Charles could never be rationalized. Besides, his intense evil ways brought fear upon anyone who would dare listen or try. When someone asked Charles, "Why do you do these things?" he replied, "Because Mary was the only person who was nice to me, and life is boring and I have nothing to do."

The FBI or Homeland Security could have used Charles at one time or another. Charles actually considered this, but these thoughts spoken were only said to appease Mary's trust and for her to bestow kindness upon his intellect. He always said things you wanted to hear, but followed the complete opposite allowing no one to ever know his true self and motives. The curtain overshadowed the true being underneath and this is how his strategy worked. Charles could have been a remote viewer for the FBI and help capture criminals by revealing their where about just by his gifted abilities. However, no one was to control Charles, no one wanted to and Charles never helped anyone as he said he would. For Charles was truly evil, with no misgivings, nor any remorse.

He had a criminal mind which took over, that which he found much amusement to perform. There was once a doctor who treated Charles in Washington, D.C. who looked at him with a magnetic glance upon first seeing Charles. As he was treating him, he saw the face of evil beaming at him.

It was then that this doctor and scientist took up a cause to defeat the power of Charles and eventually help Mary from

a distance in pushing Charles away. Mary never could meet or
really know this man's name, but she knew that he was always
present trying to fight her cause. He tried to keep Charles
from doing evil against her by much prayer and healing. All
Mary could see through her third eye was a short man with a
white lab coat. That was all that was necessary. That was all
that mattered. This doctor's help was of steadfast devotion
and persistence against a man who was evil in the world. The
evil vibrations that Charles generated by himself or through
others could not deflect the righteousness of this comrade.

Charles had assistance from his many cronies that he
incorporated in his madness. It was said that all were
hypnotized under an old Egyptian spell that only Charles
knew. All thus followed his commands and spied on those
who were family or those he did not like. These followers
were all destroyed by the good and taken down eventually,
for they spread confusion and lack of clarity to their victims.
Charles would then regroup with another group and then
another. Just as long as the job was done and that was all that
mattered.

Charles would promise these followers all a reward once
their jobs of confusion and spying had been done. Only
Charles and his assistant knew specifically what that reward
would be. The reward was one of secret powers over monies
and people. This assistant stood out above the rest. A tall,
hefty individual who was called in on specific matters that
had to do with spiraling down the victim's inertia. He made
them forever tired and not caring for the completion of any
project. He made the victim wonder on any idea why they
even started. The initial start of anything became a burden of

dismay and lethargic ruins. Mary dubbed him the Executioner. Luckily he was not used very often. Mary never ran into him on the street nor ever came face to face, but she felt his presence. It was a presence that made her feel the ever tired feeling of never moving fast or with any forward movement. This petty tyrant needed to be squashed like an ant for he threw his weight around the innocent and timid souls. And one day someone did just that. It was a victory for all that felt the weight of his injustices and the cruelty of his tricks.

At one point Charles began reading Carlos Castaneda's work called, "On the Art of Dreaming." After this, Mary began to experience dreams that were not of the ordinary. Charles would pose as people Mary knew and he reached her by her fears. One night, Charles and others were brought into Mary's dream state. The dream showed Mary that televisions were turned off and ten people were sitting watching empty screens. The ten people, unknown to Mary, pushed her out of the way so that a picture of all of them could be taken. The feat of all of them reaching Mary's dream state was too much for Mary to bear. Mary then awoke from her dream state bewildered and feeling like a large balloon was left in her head. An astral portal needed to be mended, called an "astral fracture." Mary Never saw anyone in her dreams again.

Mary was helped by a holy man who suggested removing her fears and all her insecurities attached to the fears by consciously replacing them with love and laughter. It was not easy for her to remove Charles from her psyche. He waited for her to fall asleep and would then enter into her subconscious to make sure his connection to her was never broken.

Once in awhile, Charles would bring out his large crystals and his mummified heart that was kept in a steel box. Many of these things were done by Charles through reading books and knowing those who practiced such things. As soon as a friend disintegrated and destroyed this box, heaviness and despair lifted from Mary's being. No more was she a prisoner of Zenda and nor more darkness loomed. Thus was one person of many who helped Mary.

During the midst of metaphorical trial, Mary decided to call Charles and she felt that she had made a mistake, that she may have been too hasty to turn Charles away as a friend.

"Hello, Charles, I am sorry for being too hasty. Can we still be friends?"

At that moment, Charles brought forth an anger like an angry dragon with all the fiery flames. The poison reached Mary's eyes and she could not see for three days. The burning was that powerful. Once a person makes up their mind, there is no turning back but Mary was sure that he would take her back as a friend. The anger needed to be smothered like the fire at the end of the night. This campfire had no songs being sung nor friendship shared, just burning coals of remembrance.

Charles's underlying jealousy was always the true motivation that fueled his incessant attempts to thwart the paths of Mary and others. He ran down his list, every day, of those that had caused some imaginary wrong in his life. Mary was on this list amongst those that had refused his friendship. She was at the top of his list because Charles cared for Mary in his own way. She was the only one who had given him kindness and an ear to listen.

Due to Charles's Asperger's syndrome, Charles would have an outburst of anger that manifested from a seizure or malfunction. This was uniqueness about Charles. As a child he did this to some chemical imbalance in the brain. Everyone just moved out of his way when this occurred. The energy went every which way. You may receive poison like that of a Venus fly trap or the stinging of a spider bite to the foot.

Why wasn't anyone checking on this odd fellow, like psychiatrists, clergy and social workers? Charles was a master at his work. He was able to fool the best of them by playing mind games and camouflaging himself to the point of looking like he was a poor innocent bystander, living at home with mom due to his condition. His mother, the puppet master, had adjacent police fooled with her own mind control.

"Why, she is a sweet little old lady that would never hurt or say anything bad about anyone," they retorted. Wow, were they mislead!

Mary looked for guidance in a higher power, yet on this plane she would constantly look for someone to get her away from the carnival show of Charles. Asperger's syndrome is defined as a facet of autism with the exception that although highly intellectual, one lacks social skills. This would explain why Charles would constantly read books in a very short time and was so well versed about everything. Well, almost everything. He felt nothing and looked at life as though it were a game. He would cry over things like a child, but that would stop in a very short time. This characteristic would also explain why there was no down time in all of his tortures and sufferings to others. When something that he tried would not work, he would quickly try another method, until something eventually worked. By shutting down Mary's financial world, her soul mate and work, Mary would have no one to turn to except Charles. This became his plan of execution. Although the reality of Mary never sharing a friendship with Charles was great, Charles felt that Mary may find the error of her ways and return to him, or so he thought.

Even amidst trial, Mary at times felt she was blessed and saved for a purpose. Charles was able to pass his Asperger's Syndrome, and even cancer to his victims. Mary had heard that he was able to do this, but that would not happen to her, at least not today. The thought always lingered in her mind. Mary thought at times that Charles had a cross to bear, the bearing of evil and abuse from mommy dearest. The question arose of why did Charles stay and did not escape when the time was right? The answer was that Charles's mother was the only one who understood him the most, though she was evil to the end. Yet, she was responsible for all his wrong doing, as she perpetuated his persistent evil to be done in the world.

A chip off the old block, so to speak. They were bosom buddies in crime and most would never know. However, there was one person who did know and stood far away from all of them from the very start. Mary found that Charles had a brother and this brother had nothing to do with the rest of the family. Poor soul, he knew nothing about how Charles had done something to his happy home life and that his career could have taken off in another direction if it were not for the intervention of Charles. Sometimes, it is better for people not to know what could have happened, as it wouldn't make any difference. Or would it? Mary knew and was trying to act herself, while being blocked at all attempts.

As time passed, Mary was very observant to how Charles approached his victims. His need for their energy and power was so great that he went to great lengths in order to understand how to obtain their energy. There are certain organs, for example, that represent the divine and are passageways into a person's body. First through the spleen, and then through the kidneys and to the breastbone is the main passageway. There were ways that Charles entered qigong points and meridian points from past lives that gained him entrance into the body. There was also entering the crown and higher realms, especially the fourteenth chakra that was left unattended when one was not praying all day, and alerted Charles for entrance. His scrying techniques enabled him to see where and with whom you were with for the day or hour if need be. Then, if all else failed, past lives served as an entrance for attachment together into the dream state.

Mary also was experiencing sleep deprivation, for Charles was waking her at all hours of the night, to having been raped of energy with no one specifically to call for help. When Mary was peaceful and calm, this too alerted Charles to make her angry by an energetic stream of energy he sent her way. This sounded like a high-pitched screeching noise that vibrated every part of the body. As she festered over nonsensical things or things that had already passed, Charles took over and then she became his for a short time.

Mary could not free herself, she did not know how and whoever she talked to or consulted did not know. Some people helped, like the scientist, but mainly attempts against Charles by others failed, like the shaman. There of course were those, who for a price could erase Charles, but Mary knew better that the matter was deeper than a superficial fix. An expert had to be found, but where? When Mary got too close to that answer, Charles made sure that time lapses were placed just in the nick of time to prolong that finding. He hoped Mary would give up and find another road instead in Charles's favor. That was Charles's plan.

The frustration and anguish of Mary was pushed under a carpet of dust with a broom ready to be swept away. Mary's mind became a martyr to her emotions and the sadness overwhelmed her in a sea of defeat, but Mary knew better of her never ending faith. She kept diligently following a vigilant candle flickered with a hope that someday she would be free. The echo of Charles's song, "get along little doggie," came to mind. Mary hoped that this doggie had a five hundred pound weight attached to it and the doggie would be thrown off the dock.

Chapter 5

MARY'S CRY FOR help was heard by all. Yet, no one answered the drum of her heart. She was alone in this fight against Charles. Some were too scared to help while many thought Mary deserved it for some reason or payment of some past life. However, Mary did only what she knew and that was to be kind and generous to all. Mary's friends and companions were taken away or blocked, and the tainted source of Charles left his indelible mark with coldness and fear. Some say it was sixty life times as such. Yet, the present was all Mary could withstand.

Still Mary stayed true to her faith. "I forgive you Charles, for all that you have done."

Forgiveness was not by her hand alone. A greater hand was steering her course and allowing her to see that even Charles was not led by his hand alone. All were orchestrated for a purpose.

Although a vendetta needed to be finished implicating Mary's soul mate, Charles was truly out to destroy Mary for his initial rejection of more than friendship. Charles felt no one was worthy of his love, except Mary.

As a result of Charles's love for Mary, he tried to get as close as possible to her without seeing her. He would visit her every night in her sleep and then be in her head as she awoke. He would even prey on her energy every time he could find an opening energetically.

Mary thought it best to check on her physical condition through all of this, as the spiritual can affect the physical. The doctors stated that she had osteopenia, a precursor to osteoporosis. What the doctors and Mary did not know at that time was that Charles managed to cause large holes in Mary's bone pores so that greater quantities of energy could be taken. A visit to the podiatrist also showed how energy remained stuck from the energy taken by the day, as all the residue went to her feet. Mary consulted with various healers, who brought her back to her energy, in a matter of seconds or sometimes days. Three times Mary had been close to dying but she survived. What an ordeal, but Mary was able to pull herself through to the amazement of Charles. At that point, Mary considered the dichotomy of whether to have Charles fed to the sharks or to pray for his soul and have love and laughter sent to Charles by her guides or the angels and archangels.

The seesaw of life overwhelmed her soul at times, but there was much consternation and hope that things would get better. Rebecca came back into Mary's life but was of short duration. Her road to happiness was filled with many twists and turns that she needed to solve. Life is sometimes cruel and not giving. The time comes and yet we do not always reach for the brass ring. Sometimes we think we have the answer for others, but we rarely look to our own lives. Rebecca needed help but Mary could not help her. Both remained as friends forever but the heartache of not being able to help a friend can be more disheartening than life itself. Mary bid farewell to her friend to return at a later date when Charles was out of her life. And besides, Mary did not want anything to happen to Rebecca with Charles's dark humor. The scar of Charles would try to obstruct the friendship they had. Mary wanted to keep Rebecca as a friend even if it were at a distance.

If just someone, anyone, could throw a net over this character and be done with it. However, the fear of this abomination was too great for many to attempt his guile smile and demeanor. This awkward situation held Mary captive for four and one half years, with the ever persisting Charles holding vigil on her dear life. The cronies and others exhausted her as they followed a cause that they even felt was long done with. Yet, those who are insane don't really know what they do and why they do it. They follow the drumbeat of wherever their evil leads them without forethought and usually with malice.

Mary was not free after Charles had perpetuated his trauma and these memories stayed in her subconsciously and through cellular memory. However, Mary was prepared to recover, no matter what it took. Personally, to heal, Mary had to find the answers to why all this occurred, especially when everything was going so well in her life and Ben had already taken up much of her life that needed to be discarded.

Ben had had some conscious thoughts to his malice, but Charles was naturally cruel and very evil with his thoughts to dismember his accused and torture them and in ways that he felt they needed to be taught a lesson. Women took precedent over men due to the ever-present control his mother kept over him. Sufferings and grave misfortunes happened to those who found themselves on Charles's list. His anger over mommy dearest raged inside of him, for he found her to be forever controlling and forever seeking his energy to blend with hers. These two birds of a feather found each other's company a solace that mirrored one another. They hated yet needed each other. For this alone did Charles feel something toward her, but only this.

Due to his Asperger's Syndrome, Charles was safe with her. Who but a mother would understand the true workings of their child? This grown man remained in a childlike stage that reacted to indifferences with tantrums of rage. If Charles imagined wrongs he would lash out at anyone who did not treat him with some form of kindness or compassion. While growing up, Charles was very busy bothering and teasing others who really did not know of his abilities. Charles would play with their minds and feel nothing of their consequences. He would laugh to himself; he always laughed. Maybe if they knew what was happening to them, Charles may have gotten beatings or had a few bloody noses. Perhaps this is what he needed to feel consequences and not omnipotent. Perhaps this is what may have stopped his evil ways. Matters only got worse as he got older and he never received the wallop on the head that just may have stopped his deceitful ways.

Charles began to get older and his tricks became more intense and much more sophisticated. Though very bright, he was very odd-looking and he stood out amongst others. He studied mind control to the extent of trying to change people's minds. As time went on, his thoughts and your thoughts became as one. Since no one paid attention to Charles, this was fuel for him to live by. As he read and learned about how to torture his victims, Charles would feel a sense of pride and aggression into finding devious ways to enact evil on those who did not like him. He was too frail and not combative to others, but by using mind control they were easy to manipulate and control on all who meant him harm. Yet Charles was selfish too, for he also picked on victims who were frail and innocent and would never fight back. His life then turned into one of self-satisfaction and gave him immoral strength. Yet, no one ever reported the menace that Charles had become nor did anyone ever fight his injustices. He saw to that! Their spiraling wheel of life was brought to neutralization. How could they ever dream to break from this rut?

At home he was communicating telepathically with his mother. He would bring others over and she would be in the next room listening to their every word. Her close-knit control on Charles forbade anyone to have any control over Charles. Those that entered the house of Charles had energy taken by the forces that ruled his house, mainly his mother. How Charles missed his father who was very kind and not demanding of him. Maybe he could have stopped Charles's mother from corrupting Charles. Charles was always compared to his older brother who was perfect in every way.

His brother got away, but Charles was sent off to college due to his high intelligence and remained on campus, a stone throw away from his mother's home. He did quite well scholastically, but socially he was a ring of fire, angry fierce opponent who became very cynical and hateful. He harbored this anger quite well but one could detect the anger that glared from his eyes that spoke of rage.

While in college, Charles would try to confuse and make others forget what was on their minds. Once, one of his fellow classmates wrote outside his door and then ran away: "Why the bumbling vagabonds came stumbling after like wolves following the pack. Only to find this lone wolf drawn to a thicket of thorns that entangled in his web of deception. None of the other wolves would dare go near, for they too might succumb to that state of anger, confusion and misguided array of ball of energy. They too might die a horrible death of falling upon thorns of pain. A pain that was too horrific to imagine. And a death unworthy of the cause. Now they could rest, for no longer did they have to follow the madman. No more following a possessed insane figure, whose words made them tremble with a bulliness few could defeat." His classmates never understood Charles and thought of him to be sinister and frightening. This angry message was a lasting remark that brought Charles tears to his eyes that turned to an angry revolt.

After reading this, Charles vowed to rain down fire and brimstone to those who had and would oppose his ways. He kept reading books on how to defend his evil ways and found ingenious ways to overcome his hatred for people who did not understand him. He wrote a paper once that was entitled,

"Kaunas and Their Magical Ways." He stated that there were good and bad Kaunas and the bad Kaunas can take away your wishes. Everyone smiled at him and masked their inner horror of disbelief after reading the paper, yet few could hide their true feelings from Charles.

Even though it was not of his character. Charles graduated as a public administrator who knew his job well. He continued to play tricks on those that he thought needed to learn a lesson or were in some way infringing on his personality or life in some way. In a matter of seconds, he would find one's fears and then bring it upon them. His cruel imagined indifference to those he felt jealousy or anger about caused their life to be permanently changed. The individual found that life was not how it would have been, but how Charles wanted it to be.

Yet, he never quite burned brightly as a shining star through his mother's eyes. He was only a tool. Thus, Charles never gave up his game playing in the lives of others as he got older. Charles's control as the odd fairy who changed people's life with a twisting of his hands or the slaying of his words, brought him much amusement and purposefulness.

Yet there were those who felt that his maniacal tendencies had a hole at the bottom. Brave ones decided to take shots at Charles that drove them to the brink of insanity of everlasting confusion. There had been ten assassination attempts on Charles's life that were all intercepted by the psychic ability of Charles. His inner instincts alerted him to danger and that was turned on every day and every night.

Charles had been playing his game long before he met Mary and had much experience. Where does one turn to when their life is upside down and to who does one talk to about such matters? Mary found prayer a refuge and those that understood her circumstances comforting. At times her refuge in a higher power enabled her to find peace within her mind. A holy man gave his advice and love with much inner guidance that provided a post to lean on when most troubled. However, every time Mary was happy or joyous about things in her life, an antenna surfaced to tell the world of this experience. Charles was able to intercept this and then counteract with a tower or cloud of smoke that dismantled any joy that remained.

The subconscious played a large role in Charles's hook that was buried in Mary while she was sleeping between the hours of midnight to four in the morning. He was a master of the mind by the time he attacked Mary. Deep in sleep, Mary had become submissive to a taskmaster that controlled her through hypnotic suggestion and orchestrated her power of suggestion. This implanted point of refuge kept Mary on the edge most of her waking hours. At times she was able to turn this subliminal message off, but there were times that static energy interfered along with basic interference of others and gave rise to an energy that was quick in action and too quick in thought. Charles knew this and carefully studied how to control people this way. He was a mastermind of control, the energy that he so desperately needed to make him feel empowered and of importance.

One could almost feel sadness and pity for one who would reach out for energy that would never be his, but felt needed to be taken at any cost. Part of someone's essence took the place of any love, the love he would never feel nor share with anyone. His mother saw to that!

"I don't know what drives me after Mary, I cannot control myself," he told his cronies.

They dared not talk about what they really thought of Charles. They just bowed their heads in reverence as though they felt what he had felt and continued to hear all of his story. His protective mother's love was not out of love for Charles, but a tainted desire to use him to collect energy for herself.

Mommy dearest could read Charles's mind, so why did she not put a stop to all that he was doing? Charles's mother perpetuated all that he did and worked through Charles to gain an even greater power, a strengthened will and mind. The sweet little lady of eighty packed a wallop to anyone who would attack Charles. She didn't care that her darling was taking energy, just as long as others didn't hurt him. She took energy herself. However, although Charles lived at home, he was in no comparison to his brother who was always prosperous and established. Like Cain and Abel, Charles was out to find a way to thwart his brother's life in any way possible, despite his mother's high opinion of her son.

Charles did not last long in his profession as a public administrator due to his odd behavior and lack of communication with his co-workers. After two years he decided to quit his job and become a school guard. Children would understand him and besides, Charles was able to take energy from children much more easily than adults.

Children were friendly toward Charles as a school guard and they talked to him and asked him questions. Many liked

Charles and found him amusing. He related his child-like personality to his own childhood when talking to the children and remembered how monsters appeared everywhere. He was told by his mother that they did not exist and to please stop telling lies. Although Charles's mother was able to see these monsters, she did not want to contribute to Charles's creative mind. She was a down to earth witch who wanted control over Charles's thoughts and fantasies. These monsters were the dark side's way of relating to Charles at a young age. His mother taught him many things but never knew just how truly engulfed in evil Charles was. But he knew. As Charles's creative side gave reign to monsters, his mother gave rise to teaching Charles how to defend himself because he was different. He never forgot those stories and carried them with him till he was older. Yet, Charles was afraid when he saw dark entities or dark figures. He only knew the shadow side; he never knew the light. His mother saw to that! His mother, that dark soul, never explained the light to Charles for fear of his liking.

Yet the child-like Charles continued to play with the fire of monsters up until his demise. Although he was older, in his teens, he decided to make a pact with the devil. He asked for certain favors, and his soul was then sold to the company store. These favors consisted of power over others and the destruction of those not of the shadow side. It was in his adult life that he realized that what he bargained for was not really what he wanted. It was then too late. And no matter how hard he tried to change that pact, he could not break loose from the bondage of his shadow side.

As he changed people's lives, he could never change his. For this Charles was very sad and disillusioned. We wonder why the Supreme Being allowed this being to exist, if their existence brought misery and torture to many. And yet those of the light became stronger and their light burned brighter, and everlasting compassion for the lack of light that Charles would never experience. Charles was a tool for Mary. In the scheme of things, Charles initiated a change in Mary that brought her to greater heights of spiritual obedience and growing force that changed Mary permanently. Mary found refuge in spirit and the light that enabled her to find a communication with a higher power that was burning more brightly than before. The Supreme Being works in mysterious ways. Mary had subconsciously planned the whole picture with Charles before this life and he was here to perpetuate Mary to a higher realm. Mary could not comprehend the total picture as of yet, but over time it all made sense in the scheme of things and at the end of all that took place.

Chapter 6

MARY HAD GONE through such anguish and drama that she could only feel heartache and despair. Unable to truly defend herself adequately was too much to bear. The true horror of it all subjected her faith to a greater bond with the Supreme Being and she accepted all that came to her. Charles was fighting other battles also and although Mary took precedence, she was on the back burners from time to time.

What was very hard for Mary to understand was that Charles used mind control on all her friends. Kathleen, Chris And Linda could not be touched. Their shields withstood the heaviest blows and strongest opposing forces that are amazing. However, Charles found some of her friends who were vulnerable and susceptible to Charles's attacks and schemes. Every time Mary got too close to anyone, Charles would be there to interject something that he felt could control the conversation. Mary could detect that right away and then the conversation ended. Also, what Mary could not comprehend was that Charles also had to control Mary's finances. Charles went to great lengths to find where money channels were exchanged and blocked their every move. He also tried to change peoples' mind at work about what they thought about Mary. He went into the folds of time and wrote your life the way he felt it should be written and thus Mary fought for her stability.

Sheila, through her own clairvoyant abilities, would tell Mary how to circumvent Charles's mighty blows that he sent. Sheila was a small woman with a powerful gift. Police and detective work was part of her repertoire. She also could find any poltergeist in any house or building. Mary and Sheila were very close, and Mary confided in her with just about anything. Sheila was not afraid of Charles and his cronies. Sheila also had friends that came to her aid when needed.

The sneer upon Charles's face when Sheila came to the assistance of Mary, sent Sheila into a greater conviction to destroy any bullying and controlling actions thrown at Mary and herself. Sheila had consulted with others about Charles and found him to be very dangerous. Others related to her that Charles had put an energetic wedge in someone's throat or had sent poison into someone's ear, but Sheila was not afraid. Mary related a story to Sheila that one night while she was sleeping, Charles entered her bedroom and put poison by her nose. This poison went into her lungs and could not be easily found nor seen on chest x-ray. Sheila then told her of someone she knew that could remove this.

Mary met Sheila through a mutual friend. Sheila knew they would be good friends from the start but they had no idea that they would be battling demons one time to defeat Mary and try to control her. Setting aside the thoughts of leaving town or climbing under the bed, Mary took up her amour with Archangel Michael defending her. Sheila came to her rescue by shielding her and sending the demons where they needed to go with the light.

At that moment, Mary thought about going to Charles's house and punching him in the stomach. One or two nights in jail would be well spent with the satisfaction she would receive. But no, that never took place. Mary never hit below the belt and, besides, he was too strange a fellow to even see for the fear that he might pierce her body with his eyes. Mary just closed her eyes and wished to the Supreme Being to just take him away. It was matter of believing the lies. The lies that sorcery, black magic and voodoo create, the minds that believe that it can happen. Possession of the soul could take place or control of the mind that would lead you to a dark road. Charles was believable, yet Mary's mind was much more powerful, she just didn't know how powerful enough to resist Charles. It was easy for Mary to combat Charles's anger and hatred with love and laughter, it was fear that Mary had to overcome. She was standing on unknown territory she had to master. It is not only praying to the Supreme Being that helped Mary, she began to learn universal laws and how things work around us. Standing in the light and defending the light was how Mary battled with Charles. There were others on Charles's list that Mary was trying to unite with. Possibly, Mary could tell them her story and all would work together. Unfortunately, Mary could not communicate to the others nor find them. They were all too afraid to come out of hiding. All Mary knew was that this cat and mouse game had to end, now.

Too many lives were being altered and for what? A child-like mind, playing God, or gathering up souls for the Dark One, that is the devil. Charles was so intelligent, yet did he not see that he had not grown to accept the light, or that he was a conduit for greater sources that took hold of him to do their bidding. There are two sides to everyone and Charles would hold on to the shadow side of Mary and would not let go. Mary wondered if the devil was helping Charles, and if so, how could Mary fight him then? Back at Mary's secluded library, Mary needed to think deeply about all that was taking place around her and within her. A voice whispered to go back to the time when Charles met her and remember what took place. Mary remembered that when the battle took place with Ben that she had given up her power and allowed Charles to defend her. He was jumping in and out of her body and this was the clue, the solution to Charles's energy consumption. Mary was tired of all this, and wanted answers. When she talked to the Supreme Being, no one answered. She talked to her friends for an alternate view. Yet no one could bring themselves to tell her. For Even if Mary's friends knew what was happening, no one could go to the shadow side and defend her. Once seeing Kathleen fall Under Charles's control, a malefic fear overcame Chris and Linda. They thought they too would succumb to such a fate. Sheila was the only one who, like Joan of Arc, went into the battle with Mary with no fear, no matter what the consequence.

Mary was beginning to understand that while she was being raised to greater heights of spirituality, the negativity that Charles facilitated, was being erased forever. She consulted with the Ascended Masters that surrounded her and her guides and loved ones about this new development. Mary finally understood that this was the true picture of the road she had chosen. This was the life she would remove all bad past karma. She hoped that all good karma would remain forever. She then worked with a healer named Marla who could remove her bad karma. As Charles was throwing angry balls of hatred, Mary intercepted them and turned them into a healing session that removed the past. We can take negativity and turn it into something positive. We live in the moment, yet we relive similar situations of the past until we are able to rise above the situation and make amends. Although, Mary was able to rid herself of all past lives, Charles was not going to give up his precious Mary easily. Each past life would come about when it has decided to come forward. It would come about as a whirling tornado that came from the depths of Mary, and then Marla was able to pick it up and eliminate it. Marla was given this gift to help all those who needed their past lives removed with energies that remained hidden to Mary and Marla kept to herself. This was Marla's specialty and Marla was good at what she did. Marla was a pillar of strength and well known amongst healers.

Mary was not sure how she was going to overcome this battle of wills, but she had various ideas. Charles had worked on her confidence by suppressing various points in her brain, making her weak. It didn't matter that Charles would block her soul mate from meeting her. One time during Christmas, Mary felt she would meet her true love during a meeting with an old man discussing stocks and bonds. Unfortunately, Charles energetically hit the back of her head before the meeting. The back of the head had to do with communication and signals would be crossed at the time of any meeting. There are 100 billion neurons in the cerebellum and Charles knew this. He also knew that if these neurons were cross-wired or short-circuited, then Mary would feel the effect. Once Mary entered the meeting, she couldn't wait to leave. Tears began to flow, knowing very well how important the meeting was. The white-haired man would be the person to introduce her to her soul mate. Mary quickly left the meeting and all the white haired men appeared the same. Each white haired man's face became just like another's. Christmas that Year was very lonely, especially when she saw her soul mate in Arizona, alone without her. Mary wanted to tear Charles's eyes out, but he was not around. Laughter filled Charles with victory without remorse or misgivings.

Some day, Charles would find himself alone, Mary thought. He had been alone in his thoughts all his life. Being alone conferring with himself came natural to him. Charles had been married once and found it rather a nuisance. Mary wondered who would marry Charles. Most likely, someone very confused and lonely. Mary met his wife once. She was a big woman and very round. She was the one who carried the big stick over Charles in the marriage. This made Mary wonder how powerful his wife was to keep him in place. Charles felt nothing for his wife, except a mere experience in and of itself. A lesson in life that he need not repeat. He was happy to be done with it all. Charles married a witch like his mother. His Mother approved of such a girl. She was the daughter she never had. Charles felt he could dominate Mary because she was naïve in the realm of any of his magic and, so he could surprise her in all his endeavors. Mary, although very intelligent, never dabbled in any black magic, sorcery, or negativity. She was kind, loving, and always loyal to the Supreme Being. When Charles overshadowed her light, the cloud of darkness descended with the darkest of the dark. No one wanted to go near Mary. Mary was all alone and very afraid. Fear began to creep in the very depth of her being. This is how Charles felt he could control Mary. Mary took a long time in discovering her fears and also her beliefs. And once these fears and beliefs were discovered, she needed to find if all stemmed from a past life or her current. Another healer named Rebecca worked with her from time to time on her beliefs and fears to the point of exhaustion, but all were erased and all were set free. Mary wondered about Rebecca and would see her when meditating.

Mary's friends had to warn Mary that she might go crazy if she delved too deep in matters she knew nothing about. She had to know what Charles was all about and why her nemesis had such an affinity towards her. Mary did not care what people thought of the person willing and ready to save her. Besides, Charles was working on the minds of everyone around her on a daily basis. As a form of rejection, Charles was going to change their minds through the power of suggestion and he was quite good at it. He felt Mary would see the error of her ways and return to him to stop what she had been doing, that is looking for her soul mate. Mary was very strong and not like the others that he had controlled. Mary said to herself, "I am not going to let anyone do this to me. I am a worthy person and my life is very important. I am not going to be under anyone's thumb, especially Charles's. Sick Charles who did this to others throughout his life." Mary would ask certain people who knew of these matters to try and put a net over him, or cloak her family so no one would know where she was. No one knew how to do these things, but they tried with some luck to the petty tyrant who tried to control others' worlds by his actions and pursuit. Kathleen knew of cloaking, but since she had joined forces with Charles, she used her magic for her purposes alone.

Mary, despite her utter bewilderment and horror, fought Charles with anything she knew, especially with her army of Angels, Guides and Ascended Masters. She also needed more help. Her logic was being overthrown, her whole life was being overthrown due to a rejection of a friendship with a man she knew only for a week. Mary wondered what would have happened if she had done something horrible to Charles? "I would not be alive," she thought. Sending love and blessings to a being that was turning her life upside down was not an easy feat. Healers and friends of the church prayed with Mary and advised her to approach the situation she faced. Let the Supreme Being take car of him, "Go where the Supreme Being would want you to go," they said. But Mary was physically and psychologically suffering to the point of her thinking became very murky and cloudy. She just sat and watched TV during those times, but fear ran through her spine and she wanted to know when it would end, as she asked her guides.

The fear of never reaching freedom was too much to bear. During these times one would wonder if others in various psychiatric wards underwent similar situations and whether anyone believed them? Were they given drugs to suppress their true thoughts or would they cry for help? Did

others think they had strange ideas? Charles knew very well
that he had free reign in this link of unorthodox order, his
devilish order that he ran in his mind whenever he inflicted
his evil on others. He could fool the best of them, the
psychiatrists and psychologists would never believe those he
had affected. The game of who's who was a game of expert
achievement. And Charles knew how to play this game with
much experience and with no remorse. "I appease the dark
side," he whispered to himself, and thought, "They will grant
me what I want." Even Mary could not imagine the evil
power that Charles paid allegiance to. That power was
reserved for Charles alone and he alone wanted it with all his
might. He changed people's lives by changing the folds of
time. He would first change the person's timing to throw
them off balance, then he would inflict pain and distress upon
them. He thought of himself as a god untouched! Those of
such nature leave themselves open due to their vulnerability
of thinking so. He did this all his life, and yet no one knew
the real Charles, except his dear mother. The dark suspicious
soul that she was!

Chapter 7

MARY REGAINED HER peace at times, however, Charles was hiding so he could pounce out of the blue. When attacked, Charles would step into the void, out from the light and into the dark, and no one would dare go there to close the door. The void was the absence of light and could be dark that one would have to be magical to create a door or portal and step in it. An enemy may never return. He also played possum, so that his enemy would think he had been beaten. That was a grave mistake on the opponent's part. Charles would come back with all the venom and surrounding darkness of a cape that circled with smothering dark ash. No living thing could survive. His cronies, ever faithful and fearful of Charles, listened to his command with great allegiance and faithfulness. They were all strange ones who were misfits in their own right. Yet Charles found them amusing and rather unintelligent. They never really knew what really lurked in Charles and Charles liked that very much. Charles would demonstrate his true nature when he left them dumbfounded. For that, Charles knew them well and disposed of them when the time was right. This time could never be anticipated.

Although a social worker occasionally visited Charles, he went unnoticed with his episodes of anger and frustration. From time to time, his energy would shoot everywhere, with blow-ups that were felt around the world. This emanated from Charles not taking his medication and for not controlling temper tantrums since he was small. He could never get control of his fury and madness. The sparks of red flames boomeranged from wall to wall when he entered these phases of uncontrollable rage, which made his enemies feel him as overbearing and somewhat fierce.

To Charles, everything was a matter of power, control or be controlled, conquer or be conquered. Charles only knew of survival and he was an expert at it. Charles also spent days trying to figure out how he could reach his victims if his plans failed. There was always a back up plan. Yet the arrogance of Charles continued to penetrate that small boy within. His plans failed from time to time, but he persisted with such great tenacity that his only motivation was to win. No matter what the cost and no matter how he hurt all those on his list, he had to have the last word, lashing out as best as he knew. He just had to win! How to thwart other's plans for the day and disrupt others' schedules was his plan. His cry to be heard resulted in controlling others lives and bringing them under his commands. Over time he felt he would win the game of life. But this truly became the life he chose.

The cries amongst the dark forces that ruled his world pulled on his being and ripped at his sanity and intellect with fervor and much consternation repeatedly. Yet, he did not hear the cry of all those he hurt throughout his life. A shattering of "no" never reached his thoughts. His ever persistent obsession continued in those he tortured and bullied. That swirling negative energy entered his victims with a force that no one could resist. It was a force that penetrated one's very being, to the highest and to the lowest of every pore of the soul and spirit. You became a wall of walking misalignment that resembled a modern Frankenstein with edges of darkness that reached into your body and would not let go. Your goodness was drowned out by a sea of negativity that screamed for its release. This swirling energy was a part of Charles all his life; it was a common fixture that he never thought was odd or strange. Yet, it devoured him.

Rebecca and Marla continued to help Mary to a point. When all past lives were gone and all negative belief systems had also been erased, Mary continued to need healing from the negativity that Charles had created. Mary shielded with great accuracy and helped her to realize that no one could hurt her. With no further ado, the healer stated that it would cost one hundred dollars an hour. No remorse, no feeling, no compassion. What can you say about such people? Oh, they care; on what level do they care remains to be seen. Mary often wondered what she would have done if she had not had the money to pay her, but Mary did not go there for fear of what might happen. Mary also contacted the FBI and Home Land Security in grave desperation, but all they did was take down her information and then never called her back. That would disappoint anyone in general who felt they would be on Mary's side by defending poor innocent people who were taken advantage of. Charles took advantage of unsuspecting people but careful observation would have alerted all who looked at Charles and did not adhere to that small voice inside them. Charles's eyes were evil and would send a searing energy with just a glance, burning anyone's eyes for days. Fear gripped those who thought the light was all they needed. Yet when the line was drawn, no one appeared, all had vanished. Where were all who were called upon for help; surely all her helpers could not be around to help Mary every minute or every second.

If just a hundred followers of the light stood against this dark lord, then the boastful braggart would fall to pieces and none would speak his name ever again. Bring down the abomination, Mary cheered, but no one listened, all shuffled away in fear. Mary will divulge this illusionary magician and display his gaudy showmanship to all, yet that would not happen today for some time. Prayer was kept vigilant in hopes that someday that would be true. There would be no peace until Mary could live without the whispers and thoughts of Charles. She prayed that would be soon. Charles liked this game and each day was a challenge to live another day to try to take control of Mary. Each day she thought she was getting closer to her freedom, while Charles knew better. Each day he would continue to try something new and keep all pieces on the chess- board from moving.

As the weeks went by, it was time to be creative and find those who might listen to Mary and her predicament. It was time to seek paranormal groups or people who might listen to reason about such a thing. Chris, Linda, Marla, Sheila and Rebecca could only reach their limits and the ever-persistent

Charles kept inventing new ways to attach to Mary. Other than her friends, no one was going to listen to Mary at this time, so she decided to uncover all who might shed light on the abomination, Charles. No one wanted to listen, and if they did, there were strange looks that resembled the stares of a passerby at a hospital for the mentally insane. One truly needs to be careful when talking about psychic or abnormal occurrences. Although Mary always had this lofty idea that there was only light, she was rudely awakened to the fact that there are two sides to everything. She became much more tuned with the world with a greater understanding. Darkness looms in places that we never imagine it to be. Mary never really knew where dark and devious Charles was, but at times she knew that her light would dim when Charles made his presence known.

Charles was ever trying to keep vigilant watch over those he felt he could bully and control. Mary was not versed on such matters of the dark, even though it was discovered that some of Mary's past lives were very dubious and slippery. It was only after she had talked to a past life regressionist that it became known that Ben was her child in a past life when she was a male, and that she had killed him as her son. Charles was another child in Mary's past lives that had died and she could not save. Mary was positive that Charles had known this without delay. Mary quickly got on her knees and asked the Supreme Being for forgiveness and atonement was granted. Charles was ever persistent in his pursuit with Mary. He entered each past life in hopes to control Mary no matter what. As all these past lives started to rise within her, Marla, healer and friend, would take them out one by one. Each was accompanied by a tornado and at times, blocks of cement that needed to be blasted from her being. Mary began to feel lighter and Charles could not attach himself in any way to his precious Mary. Once a past life is lifted, it can never come back, and the past people could never enter your life again. This pleased Mary, but Charles would enter a tirade of rage and anger at this, followed by smoke and brimstone.

As time passed, Charles became increasingly jealous and continued to plot and scheme to shut down all avenues of Mary's life. He felt that if he could work on the minds of people where she worked, that would make it difficult for her to stay there and, in turn, they would not want her. Despite Mary's good efforts, she was finally let go and she was devastated. As she gathered her things, the others sneered and looked askance. It is then that Mary knew Charles was responsible. There was also a distinct odor present, much like Charles.

Mary had few friends outside her healer friends, and Mary noticed they were also beginning to look with hesitation. One night, a friend called and stated that she was experiencing stomach problems and a strange feeling. Mary understood and consoled her, "Better get some rest, it's probably something you ate or it is in the air." But Mary knew that Charles had gotten to her and she began to panic. These antics that Charles executed kept Mary on her toes and also very diverted from her soul mate. Charles was far too organized and clever to let his modus operandi be known. After some time, one could figure out what he was doing. But by that time, his plan had happened and the damage was done. The smell was a dead give-away, especially when Mary would put a particular perfume on and then two days later the smell would reappear around her. The deep-seated anger and jealousy of Charles manifested in an ever persistent objective in accomplishing his goals to destroy Mary, even if it takes her to be penniless and begging. Mary prayed that would not happen and, of course, she kept all roads to idea for a better tomorrow. His ever-present energy that surrounded her never allowed her to be free. The energy of Charles was heavy and scratchy with gravitational pulls of a black hole. The emptiness that Charles felt diverted him to pull the happiness and joy from others and thus he felt happy in his own right. For why should anyone be happy when he was not? What did he have to be happy about? It sounded a bit like the "Grinch who Stole Christmas." If he had Mary as a prisoner that was really not what he wanted. But his joy in hurting others and having control over them gave him a dark sense of humor and cynicism only he could enjoy. The horror of it all reverberated in Mary's mind.

Mary tried to investigate if there had been other people like Charles in history. She could find none. However, through a link of a person named Jeremy who knew of such things, she discovered that there are four other people in the world similar to Charles. Mary tried to find them but none were recorded anywhere, or least if they were recorded or talked about none were to be found. Yet Jeremy searched for those of the dark and they knew where others could be found, just by tapping into their telepathic and psychic abilities. A clone of Charles was quite frightening. The group's name was Called Aloscha, a motley crew of undesirables who felt they wanted power and could access this power through their minds and extract evil thoughts for their own purposes. That was clearly frightening. It is the intent of evildoers that manifests great power. Underneath the rough veneer of Charles lay an innocent child unsure of his emotions. Yet, he continued to feel some closeness to Mary, since Mary showed an act of kindness towards him. Not even his family, or for that matter his mother, ever touched him like Mary. Mary the innocent by-stander who treated everyone as though they were family.

To others, he was an object of strange ridicule for his feminine characteristics and his odd evil look that stood behind a wall of angry jealousy and hatred of those who got too close. Charles's feminine characteristics were adapted when he mimicked and adapted to his mother's influence. In this way he acted her authoritarian ways and made fun of her scolding upon him. His twenty personalities developed to free himself of who he wanted to be or could not express.

There is always darkness and light and one cannot exist without the other. In all probability, Charles was the imbalance of a greater evil and a flicker of light. His desperate reaching for what he never had was sincere, but he never reached the depth of what is ordinarily easy for others. His silent desperation grew to a point of nonexistence and, then completely disappeared from sight. The figure of the man was taken over by dark forces that controlled his very being. His obsessiveness was a cry to be heard at all cost, no one was listening. The jealousy and anger rose from the everlasting flame that tried to put out the glowing ember of success and happiness.

Mary, with the help of Rebecca, Chris, Linda, Marla and Sheila, underwent a constant clearing and healing. This gave birth to a new way of looking at life and the emergence of hopes unseen. At times, she would spiral down to a never-ending spiral that never topped. Charles was constantly trying to bring down haughty Mary with pompous egotism and conceited ways. Charles relied daily on his cronies to send vibrations of confusion and disarray.

Charles could count on the cronies and if they decided to disobey, he would send a sixteenth century witch after them to change their minds. The arrogance Charles displayed reached to the depths of hell and to the highest heights his soul could reach. "No one can touch me, just let them try," he boasted. But who was listening?

His cronies just scoffed and sneered underneath to mask what they really felt. Charles was a lost soul that felt he needed to teach Mary and her soul mate a thing or two. He wanted them to remember and see that he was the boss and He ruled over them. Besides, no one is going to take his Mary away from him, even if Mary and her soul mate were meant to be together. "Just let the Supreme Being bring them back together after I'm through with them," he muttered to himself. His evilness was a persistent rage day after day until all knew who was in charge. No one stood in the way of Charles. He was running wild in the streets. Who cares for such creatures? They act and do as they please, for no one, except his cronies, could stand to be around him. Their fears held them prisoner of an entity that mimicked curiosity towards things they could hardly imagine to be true. The cronies fears helped them be prisoner of an entity, a crazed diabolical character, that peeked their attention toward things they could hardly imagine to be true. They continued to follow without hesitation or argument due to the large demon that kept them in line.

Chapter 8

MARY DECIDED TO seek help from various organizations that were well versed on Asperger's Syndrome to see if she could find any answers and, maybe, help to institutionalize Charles. All Mary found were disbelief and astonishment at Charles's behaviors. The responses she received basically stated, "What would you like us to do?" The experts just looked at her shock and dismay and avoided her call for help with Charles. "We are busy," and "We would have to see this fellow in order to pass a firm diagnosis." Mary knew that this was not going to happen. She was shocked and defeated as another avenue closed. However, she would not give up. One should never give up whenever fighting for any cause, they just need to have perseverance and conviction to stand up for what they know is right and not let anyone bully them. Especially, a character like Charles, who was playing with peoples' lives as though it was all a game of chess. Mary wanted to shake them all and make them listen to their own absurdity and chaos. Mary had four hundred Angels, Guides and Guardians on the other side, helping her, pushing her and wanting her to succeed over this abomination. It was Mary's duty to call upon them and ask them for help. We all need to ask for help and they will listen and help from the other side. She would speak to them on a daily basis and they would assist her. There were other times Mary would just ask those on the other side to protect all that she knew, and to send her angels to Charles to direct him to the light. She did not doubt because when you doubt then nothing happens. Your intent has to be one hundred percent pure in order to accomplish all that you want to accomplish. That also holds true to things we do or say every day. Forgiveness was also present in Mary's mind. She read many books on forgiveness but she could not bring herself to this now.

Meanwhile, Charles had schemed for quite some time with great care on how to pull Mary down on every avenue he could. The persistence with which he daily gave attention to his grand scheme was almost ingenious. Almost, that is. There were others, from Mary's point of view, who were helping Mary overcome his moves.

Although Charles would take energy from the "divine" spleen and then go through the kidneys and liver, up to the breastbone and out, he would not be able to take energy from Mary anymore. Mary was shielded from any interference, which made her less susceptible to an attack from Charles. Mary's soul mate, on the other hand, was very vulnerable. He would continue to ask himself, "Why is this happening to me? I am a good person and this sort of thing is not fair. Who, but the dark forces, would be coming after me?" Little did he know that Charles was the negative influence that tried to separate from Mary. That heartless Charles, that soulless being! No remorse, just a giggle or two to remind him of how clever he really was. Occasionally, he thought of his victory over Ben. Ben was overcome with schematic technique and a lot less flare.

There were those who helped Mary for obligations of friendship and nothing more. And there were those who wanted a great deal of money to erase her sorrow. No one knew just how they made up these prices, but Mary gave ear to their opinions. What Mary was not aware of was a particular holy and powerful person who she consulted from time to time that decided to secretly work against her. This holy man decided to put a golden cage around Mary. This golden cage would encircle Mary and only allow her to do those things the holy man wanted her to do. If Mary disobeyed, then Mary was punished by something bad happening to her. Thus Mary believed that her spiritual strength was weakened and reverted to feel humble and return to the holy man for help. This false prophet duped many with his humble Indian ways and it all ended with monies needing to be given for salvation and redemption. One day, Mary was alerted by Sheila as to this false prophet's deceptive veil. Mary thought all that this holy man sent would be sent to him tenfold. Yet Mary felt sadness for those that stoop to such deception. Their evilness falls on them eventually for all to see and hear.

Kathleen had come to mind and Mary felt how evilness can envelope others. These buttons of spirituality were pushed to a point that Kathleen could never recover. But

Kathleen found Mary as a naïve empty soul who would believe anything. When Mary suspected Kathleen's underhanded nature, she quickly cut off any correspondences and closed the door to a once trusting friend. May the door be ever closed to this drowning soul that will never be opened nor relived. Mary's greatest fear was that she would not be free, ever. We all need freedom to be ourselves. We should appreciate our freedom of self and all that we stand for. The courage to say and express who we are is important. Mary felt none of this as Charles's bullying kept her chained to the Devil as though she were Persephone for six months and was allowed to surface to this world only for the other six months. The ever persistent battle of Charles trying to keep Mary's soul chained was too much for Mary to bear. Mary had to find a way to free herself from those who rode with great strides of jealousy. Mary's energies were stuffed in a box that was ready to spring up as jack-in-the-box, but would never be allowed to do so. At times, Mary was the chariot rider with the reins of the light on each side with whoever was in the middle. The middle pie of existence.

Mary decided to move and try to find an existence far from where she lived now. It didn't matter where it led her, she needed to move away from all this confusion and restraint that Charles had flung in her direction.

Doreen was another friend of Mary's that was short lived. For one month, Doreen helped Mary with her chakras, swirling energy circles of the body, but Charles was too strong and overcame her. Doreen also was looming with thoughts of jealousy and hatred in comparison to her false-mirrored life that gave birth to more of the same misery.

Charles continued to use Doreen to seek vengeance and suffering until Doreen could not be used any more. Her own seeds of jealousy gave way to the shadow side of her soul. Doreen portrayed the all-powerful example of light that tried to be all that people spoke of. One night, Doreen's anger and jealousy rose to the height of Charles's control. Doreen did not fight it and it resulted in a flat-line. Gone was her life, and gone was her might. The faithless friend who masqueraded as a helpful soul really Enacted a play that found herself circling her victim with a vengeful anger to obstruct and bring ruin to everything. Charles also had enemies that were nearby or far away, as Mary was told. From time to time this helped in Charles remaining distant from Mary.

Mary decided to take another route and this time she felt that not only were there past lives to be erased with Charles, but she needed to resolve past lives within herself that attracted these things in the first place. When the student is ready, the teacher will appear. She came into contact with a Man named James who helped her with this issue. He began to dismantle Mary's psyche to find her true self buried underneath. In two hours, he began a journey of incomprehensible stature that even Mary was quite amazed with.

He first started by changing and eliminating synapses, connections of the nerves, in the bottom of the brain, by making them all new and shinny. There was a black snake in Mary's spine with eggs. An implant that was long in stature, and from a being from the beyond long ago. An etheric hole, energy surrounding the body that was found on the left side of the head. Fifty African tribesmen that Mary had contracts with and had used her as a sacrifice, was swept away by the Ascended Masters of this world. A rope was tied to Mary's foot long ago by small people who came from a country that was very cold. Mary was a child whose mother had defended her during times of abuse. All were dissolved. James found a hole in the chest that was also dissolved, an etheric hole that needed to be closed. Fifty orbs were taken out of the solar plexus in the stomach area. The orbs were small round balls of energy placed there for some reason. Crystals in the third eye, the space in the forehead between your two eyes, had been darkened for one reason or another were taken out. Mary Was not told about the other crystals that were also taken out. Two snakes, one green and one black, were removed from Mary's DNA. These were placed there by two aliens. There had been trauma to the chest from long ago that was also repaired when Mary had died as a child from several beatings. All were repaired. Pressure in the brain and nose were released in balloons. When people think negative thoughts or negative things about you with ill intent, hooks, swords, or knives are sent to your body. James claimed that Mary's body was covered in such things, things not seen with the naked eye. Her left foot had much poison and needed repair. All was much better after James had done his work. The miracle worker proceeded on. An old witch was attached to Mary, trying to bring forth her power in this life. James closed that door never to be opened.

Chains, golden armor, and steel surrounded her heart placed there by others. All had taken off and repaired. Small demons were pulling on a chord that was attached to her right foot. This link, too, was severed and gone forever. Heart

Murmur repaired. And if that was not enough to bring relief, a Susqechewan, a big foot, was attached from birth who loved her and kept close to her body. It was told to go on and that this was not the place to be. Mary felt lighter after all that had been done and much clearer to all that was removed. To her amazement, she wondered how she could have carried all these things with her all this time.

Mary believed that all disease emanates from the spirit and then floats down into the physical. Disease manifests the same as life from heaven down to earth. There are many today who say the battle in heaven starts with angels and demons and then floats down to our world. Mary just thanked The Supreme Being for James that he was able to do such work. Mary never heard from James again. He was whisked away to others' needs, as so great they were.

The ever-present jealousy of Charles perpetuated his whole being. His whole being churned with great strides of venom and hatred for those who found him repulsive and unlikeable. He was a dark poetry in motion with a twist of cynical sarcasm that dripped from his smile. His fiendish plots revolved around the every pursuit of Mary, who he felt was his alone and no one else's.

Mommy was gravely ill and Charles needed to be at her side. Even though she was about to die, she kept Charles near her to take whatever energy she could from him. Although, he felt no remorse or compassion, Charles knew that the one person who knew him well was dying. Mommy told Charles that she would contact him on the other side and he could always connect to her energy if need be. Charles, for some reason, felt that he was losing his only world and began to weep. He wept for a long time until she finally passed away that day. Upon her death, he went mad and started screaming. Many of his cronies consoled him, but they could not relieve his heartfelt attachment to his mother, despite all that she had done to him. The rest of the family came by to suppress the cries, but few could console his attachment to his older female version that knew him well.

Due to having Asperger's Syndrome, the family decided to ship Charles off to relatives to keep him quiet and at peace. He went to Washington to be near a distant aunt who consoled him. But Charles was ever anxious and very sad. "Why is this happening and why couldn't I save her?" he thought. All the Energy that he gave to her could not save her. The energy Charles gave her was very great, yet after her death his sanity began to spiral downward. His soul could not permit him to reach higher heights with the ever-present demon within. "I will miss her and I know she will always be with me," he said to himself. All his anger towards her vanished and all his internal churning about her misgivings ceased. Charles felt as if he had died with her and for the most part he had. One month after her death, he began to grow angry and evil. "Who would do this to her?" he screamed. "God did this to her! Now, I will seek vengeance with the Devil to fight all those that oppose me."

The Supreme Being heard him, all right. But the Supreme Being did not answer. And Charles could not relate to the Supreme Being for he knew nothing of these matters. His nose and face were forever turned towards the ground, cursing All who got in his way and whoever looked at him. Charles did have feelings for his mother, even though he was greedy for her money left after her death. He would never forget her or her ways. She lived on through him, and every once in a while would shine down on Charles to let him know that she is there for a little while.

Meanwhile, Mary would keep track of Charles's every move along with others. It is always good to keep vigilant of your opponent's moves, so that there are no surprises. Mary would take up her armor daily. And, daily Charles would silently attack or change something in Mary's life energetically to keep Mary guessing. It became a Hatfield and McCoy battle, but with less bickering and more continued onslaught. Mary became weary and tired of "all this stuff," as she put it. Yet, games increased with an absurdity that had no rhyme or reason of any sort. Mary recalled being awakened one night at two a.m. by a voice that loudly vibrated, "Oh, Mary, what are you doing?" Mary was frightfully shivering but answered, "Oh, Nothing!"

Mary held on with all her might and would not give in. Charles could not believe how Mary withstood all that he did without giving up. She was also fighting for all those he had afflicted, not to mention her soul mate too. There was no turning back and giving up. He would keep an energetic block to all that were destined to come near her. If there were any court money or anything coming by carrier, he would find a way to bypass the main route and carry it to an unknown destination. He would work on the minds of those sending money to her by causing great affliction or disruption. And this disruption would cause fighting and bickering to those involved with any of her money. It was a sight to behold! Jobs were a different matter. For every time she applied to a job, she was turned down or the job was withheld for lack of funds or some other reason. That too was a sight to behold, for who would imagine anyone going to such lengths to control a person? Only Charles held that position and would only step forward to the plate.

There was another holy man who spoke the truth and walked that truth. Mary would see him now and again. He gave Mary hope when there was none. This holy man explained to her that she kept herself in bondage because she believed the lies of evil. Mary did not understand this. Fear, depression and sadness keeps us in bondage, which Charles knew so well. Mary just wanted to be with her soul mate and would not listen. This is what Charles counted on. Charles would pay visits to the holy man at night to tempt him in his vices, but one should not tempt a holy man. The holy man had far more important things to do than listen to foolish Charles and his playful ways. Charles was so intelligent, yet, he could not reason with what he felt and what he knew to be so. His rationalization kept him a prisoner of his mind.

He tried to do this and that to others, but since his mother's death, all had turned on him, giving him a taste of his own medicine. Mary was persistent in prayer, and wanted nothing to do, say or want from Charles, except her soul mate who was patiently waiting for her when all is done. When one door is closed, another was waiting for Mary to walk through. We are all prisoners of our fears; it is when we look at them at their worst that we are able to distinguish them. Discipline, in all that we say and do, keeps us ever aware of our lives and allows us to overcome many a trouble. Charles would also affect and check on Mary's spiritual devotion and alignment, for when she was low in faith, he became more aggressive and more controlling. His visits to her higher realm gave way to a negative avenue when not guarded or closed.

Chapter 9

ONE DAY, MARY could not take any more of Charles's badgering and energy attacks and decided to travel. During one attack, Charles came to Mary while she was sleeping and energetically placed poison by her nose. Although the poison went undetected at the hospital, Mary was able to find a healer who could remove such things. She was not in any position to go after Charles at this time unless she regrouped and knew how to overcome the basis of this mishap. Just maybe, she would find someone in a distant land that might rescue or save her from this beastly being. As energy travels anywhere you go, the farther Mary went, the less Charles could reach her. Although Charles knew where Mary was, his energies could not reach that distance. Mary decided to visit a friend in Japan and to her, that was far enough. People were so friendly there and many would greet her with open arms. She decided to stay with someone in Kyoto. A friend gave her money because she felt Mary needed some rest and relaxation. After arriving at her destination, she could no longer feel Charles. One week went by and still, Charles could not be felt.

Her real peace came when she decided to climb Mount Fuji. Monks residing on top of this great mountain talked to her for some time. The end of Charles was imminent and his thoughts could not reach her thoughts. All was serene and at a standstill. The monks gave her advice and told her that in order to reach enlightenment, one has to rise above such matters, the matter Of Charles and his negativity, and free their soul, even if bound by their shadow. Mary could not believe her ears. She didn't realize that Charles was making her wallow in her own misery. Mary no longer wanted to feel bad about herself, nor did she want to continue being a prey in Charles's plans. The riddle of her life became clearer, but she still could not release herself from this hazy fog that encircled her without an escape. She came down the mountain with a ray of hope that she had at least found some answers.

Taking hold of Mary and her soul mate's will was not an easy task, especially when both are strong willed. Charles would chord into their solar plexus and extract energy from both. He wanted to bring Mary and her soul mate to their knees in their own unique way. Mary had heard of a young man that Charles tried to transfer his Asperger's Syndrome to. "Maybe I would not have it anymore," he muttered to himself. Although, partially successful, this young man was able to avert the danger. Charles, the man in the bubble, needed to be supervised for he inflicted his manipulative schemes on the innocent. The innocent could not believe the things happening to them. Perhaps, they would think that they were suffering from some inexplicable malady. As time went on, Charles's effects on many became visible. They would walk differently and look like they were dazed and bewildered. They also could not think clearly or were drained looking. Charles did not care, he thought only about bullying and being in control. Control of his world alone.

Where were all the seers and those with the ability to see beyond who could help Mary? Everyone knew about Mary's dilemma, but appeared distant when the question was asked. The way to overcome Charles was seen by many but few would undertake such a matter for all could not believe his evil and despicable ways. No one gave Mary any hope that she would overcome Charles. Yet, her prayer never ceased and comforted her through all. How could anyone not tell Mary that she was tied to her shadow side? For those on ventilators, do we not whisper to them and tell them that they will be all right despite all that they are under? Do we not want them to recover no matter what the odds are? Despite all that was being done to Mary, no one found it their place to tell her what was going on. Therefore, Mary became angry with all. She needed to know, and needed to know right now. Her life was in the hands of a madman and no one would tell her why. Be gone all seers, be gone all telepaths, and be gone all clairvoyants! Be gone all you hoodlums of mystic ways who fanatically rob you of hope and justice. When answers didn't come to Mary, all kept silent and vanished before her. Those creepy crawlers of life who sneak under carpets and behind creaky doors never could be found. Let karma come back to you tenfold and may the person you rob come back to rob you. Mary's pain and anguish became a liberation. Her faith in herself and her spiritual faith overcame all that tried to hurt her.

They say that in everything we say or do, there's a lesson to be learned. A lesson that sometimes, one might not want to face. Mary asked herself many times, was this her lesson? Do we not listen to the small voice that tells us what to do? Was this all about power? Was this about rising above our mundane life and reaching for a higher consciousness? Or, was this all about getting closer to the Supreme Being and keeping our faith forever steadfast and vigilant? These answers did not come easily.

At the same time as all this confusion with Charles, there were other webs of deceit being sewn by others who thought Mary was a threat. Their reflections were of a black rose withering with much disappointment. Yet, their craftiness brought them to greater heights of power. Mary worked with an aloof woman who was in a position of authority and who remained aloof to her real identity. Behind her ghastly sneering was a well organized imposter of life. Out of jealousy for Mary, She would secretly perform voodoo against Mary. Mary was told by a close friend of this woman, that she had been doing this for quite some time and that Mary was her latest victim. She was ignorant of all her wrongdoing and in thinking that she could accomplish all that she set out to do. Mary saw her evil ways and so did all those who truly watched out for Mary. The woman masked her insecure worth and placed her whole being on putting others down. "There would be no light outshining me," she thought.

Mary's light that had been dimmed by Charles just waiting to be brought out shone from within. We live in a world that one needs to be protected from those who cast evil as though it were some folly of power that gives them reign over others. For such, their house is brought down upon them sooner or later. This house is one of destruction and backward motion. The spit they spew comes back to hit them. Yet some continue to do such things until one day far into the future, they see a wrinkled and disfigured soul that cannot rise above their own matter. This is the evil that one cannot forsake or have rendered.

Mary moved far away from this misguided soul and found refuge in her life, free of such people. Charles, on the other hand, continued to think about his attack on those he imagined had done him wrong. As he leaned back in his chair of contemplation, he devised a plan so devious that he was surprised. "Ah, this is how I will do it," he remarked. Charles decided to use mind control on those that surrounded Mary at work, leisure activities and at home. He thought, "No one can come near her, I will persist. I will push them away every time I see anyone going near her," he told himself. "This way she will be all alone. As for her job, I will create havoc around her. As for her soul mate, others will take her place. I will see to that. And each facet of her life I will affect until she screams for help. And then, she will find the error of her ways, and come home to me." Charles even went as far as to have her soul mate's friends talk bad about Mary, although, he had not known people at work to speak badly about finding someone like Mary. Mary was fraught with disheartened rage and sadness.

How anyone could go this extreme was beyond anything Mary could imagine. The depth of Asperger's Syndrome was yet to be found. Science needs to find out what those with this particular syndrome can accomplish, good or bad. Charles had gone so long without being detected that Mary thought he just might never be found! Charles learned all this from his mother, that darling soul! The unsuspecting, merciless soul who looked as though she could not hurt a fly. But evil lurks in strange ways. She taught him everything in addition to others who gave him specific training at a very young age.

Time lapses were of greatest concern to Mary. Charles was able to take a part of your life's time and manipulate or postpone all that was going to happen to you. This explains why Mary would see things happening to others but not to her. They were moving forward while she stayed stationary. Mary had to remember that the Supreme Being was ultimately in charge and that her faith was severely tested. During a crisis it is important to remember that all is not lost and remember No one has any power over you no matter what fear you hold. Her soul mate was there waiting and Mary would not let him succumb to the evil waves of Charles, no matter what it took. And what propelled Charles to keep perpetuating these acts that he had to win the game and take Mary's life and to destroy any happiness? This happiness was never felt by Charles and this is what festered in his gut and his jealousy continued to overpower him. His Draconian laws were applicable to all on his list and Mary was no exception. Mary kept re-reading, "Universal Law for the Aquarian Age," by Dr. Frank Alper, (1986):

"Negativity is a balancing expression of the love vibration designed to expose the soul to the spectrum of

frequencies involved within an action and a reaction. It is of
the importance that all of my children understand the role
that the laws of negativity play in your life, in your growth,
and in your evolution. No soul involved within a karmic
pattern of growth can achieve communication and oneness
with the Father unless it has passed through the Laws of
Negativity and assimilated them. This is Law. The basic
problem is that most humans relate to negativity as
something evil, as something detrimental and to be avoided at
all cost. It is time for mankind to understand that negativity is
merely a balancing expression. It is a lower vibration of Love,
but it is a vibration of Love, for that is all there is. The most
important Universal Law is that all, and I stress all, is always
in 'Divine Order.' What does this mean to you? It means that
here are no 'accidents' relating to your true, spiritual
existence. It means that everything takes place in your life
exactly at the time it is to occur, and in the capacity and
degree to which it is meant to occur. If this were not so, the
vibrations within any given situation on any planet, solar
system, or galaxy would be thrown out of balance. This
cannot be allowed to take place."

These words justified Mary's being and allowed her to
see her situation in a different light. It sounded a lot like a
Beatles' song. Mary tried to envision this and hope that she
overcome all of Charles's negativity. Yet there was doubt, and
there will always be doubt gnawing at us. It was all too unfair
to Mary. Let Charles go bother anyone but her. The suffering
was too great. Let us bring the house down on his head and
all others who cause misery to another. What shame are those
who seek money for other's suffering! Mary's words were

spoken with much tenacity and much anger. For all who had bargained with Mary, no one got to the heart of the matter except two people. Many who posed as healers, prolonged her suffering for their own benefit, mostly financial. Those clever souls! They will pay for that. Few escape the suffering for condemning those who mean well. Mary knew that these clever souls succumb to an inevitable fate of hardship.

Mary decided to move from her house which turned out to be the right choice. A man came to her house to investigate any paranormal activity. He found out that the house was built in the 1600's when there were many pirates, Native American Indians on the land within a five-mile radius. Underneath the house there was a stream that led to an underground cave where many Indians and pirates were buried. Mary then decided to move off the land, not only because of the Indians and pirates, but because Charles and all who did not like Mary made her an easy target there and that was enough to run and never come back. There was also a question of robbers and a chest of gold nearby, but Mary did not care and it was time to leave.

After leaving, Mary became happy, and for one month, she was at peace. After two months, Charles looked desperately for her and traced her steps to her place where she was before. He found her after three months and began to bother her once again. For those three months, she was in heaven without any anxiety or restless sleeping that plagued her when Charles and his motley crew bothered her with such persistency and ridicule.

With much confusion and much disarray, Mary was affected by Charles and his cronies. By keeping Mary

confused and going around in circles, Charles and all others
would keep her off her track. Charles, with all his bullying
had the upper hand for now. Were there no others who
combated with Charles? Where were the others on his list?
Was Mary the only one combating Charles? The others were
never found, but they were mentioned. All were under the
cloak of confusion and bewilderment, never knowing what or
who was affecting their lives. Oh, how Mary wished she
could find them and combat this abomination together. Mary
even wondered if anyone survived the attacks and if they
were sane? Mary to this day doesn't know. But one night,
Mary felt their cry. It was great and nothing could silence it.

A dear friend of Mary's, Sheila again, would comfort
Mary. And from time to time, Linda and Marla would come
to the rescue. However, Sheila would always combat Charles
and his crew with everlasting heroism and bravery. Mary
would relate in messages all that was being done by Charles
and Sheila would secretly reverse all that was being done.
Mary knew she could rely on Sheila at any time or any place.
The two were inseparable. Although Sheila could not save
Mary from Charles and his crew, she was ever vigilant in
trying to overthrow their assaults and tried desperately to find
a way to hinder their Progress. Sheila had the stature of a ball
of fire with dark eyes and profound characteristics. She was
short but she proudly demanded attention when she walked
in a room. She was Mary's "seeing eyes" that looked within
for answers and never relied on others for guidance. Only
Sheila knew of these matters with Charles to let Mary know
what was happening. Sheila could not predict what was
presently churning in Charles. Charles was unpredictable and

very surprising. He was a magician of the dark arts. Who could ever find the true Charles wrapped in layers of dark smoke and everlasting deceit? Sheila was Mary's only true friend who never spoke in judgment and only she understood what Mary was going through.

Sheila had also taken many blows from Charles and needed reinforcement. Sheila had many friends who came to her rescue and she was known as the remover of poltergeists of unfamiliar territories. She was a strong adversary in her own right and no one ever crossed her path. Sheila remained forever faithful with tears of joy and laughter whenever she and Mary would talk or meet. Mary knew she was family from the day they first talked and nothing was going to change that, not even Charles.

Chapter 10

CHARLES CONTINUED TO live off his mother's money and continuously waged war against anyone who infringed on his demeanor. One day, he started to feel a sense of confusion. He decided to go to the doctor and find out what could be causing such a problem. The doctors gathered around him and told him that he had an inoperable heart valve problem and that he could die tomorrow or live for many years to come. He took the news rather well and decided to hope for the best, but he knew that time was ever ticking and that he may be here for only a short time. He never told the others and found that he was trying to find ways to compensate for all that he had done to others.

This was a strange phenomenon and his crew could not comprehend it. Charles was afraid of dying and he was afraid of being punished for all he had done. No one could believe his change of heart. All his life, Charles had done evil and changed people's lives. His new sickness had changed him. There was hope in his consciousness. He signed on the dotted line with the Devil knowing his life would be damned forever. Such strangeness enveloped his being. He was caught in between his righteous soul and his evil soul. He was fraught with what he knew to be right, which he had fought against all his life. Charles went away that day after the diagnosis knowing that he had to make a decision about his direction even though he was at crossroads of despair. He thought about Mary every day, he would not let her go. And that was his final decision. It was to the death. His evil ways would not let go, and besides, his twenty personalities continued to restrain anything in Charles that allowed him to reason or embark on a path of possible less darkness.

As his heart became weaker, he had acts of rage and violence frequently. There were times when Charles wanted to turn a new leaf, but he was not permitted by the oath he had taken. He never truly came to terms with the news of his heart, in hopes that if would stay dormant or perhaps he could buy time with whom he had bargained with to stay on earth a little longer. A mentor of his was in the hospital at the time of his news. This man taught others in the neighborhood how to be evil and combat other evil beings. To Charles's surprise, he was dumbfounded by what he saw. His mentor suffered a brain aneurysm and could not remember who he was. Upon hearing this, Mary wondered if people who do evil as Charles had succumbed to the same inevitable fate of something appearing in the head instead of the heart. No one will ever know. But Charles knew and he became afraid for himself. The clock kept ticking much louder than before. As John Donne remarked, "Never send to know for whom the bell tolls, it tolls for thee," Charles thought. No one would be there for Charles. His mother warned him of such things. His mother knew him well.

That night Charles had an all-telling dream. He saw himself as a very poor child in India. He was sent back and forth from family to family until he was bought by a family in America, in his later teen years. Charles, as he awoke, found this very alarming. He realized at that moment that the dream indicated his evil ways. In his next life, he would lead a life of confusion and hardship due to the suffering he had caused in this life. The question arose, would he change his evil ways after what he had seen? "Again, when the wicked man turneth away from his wickedness that he hath committed, and doeth that which is lawful and right, he shall save his soul alive. Because he considereth, and turneth away from all his transgressions that he hath committed, he shall surely live, he shall not die." Ezekiel 18:27-8 KJB

Charles continued on his path of destruction to hurt Mary emotionally and financially without any remorse, and others who followed were overcome by fear and regret. The others knew that they too would succumb to such a fate if they continued on their evil ways. Only Charles's assistant decided to stay, for he was loyal to the end. If he only knew that Charles felt nothing for him and that he would be disposed of as quickly as he would say hello. The assistant fed off the energy of Charles and without Charles, he would be a blade of grass in the forest. "Get along little doggie," Charles sang. Only Charles knew what was in store.

Mary decided this time to visit a friend in New Zealand. This time, many got together to help Mary because they knew she needed an answer and gave her money to make the journey. Although it was quite far, Mary knew she could find peace of mind there and some calmness within her being. Her friend's name was Mark and he had this uncanny way of talking and being a friend to Mary. He would occasionally take walks with Mary that allowed both of them to contemplate their direction in life. Mary called this her "walkabout."

Mary did not worry about Charles here because she was so far from home and could not be reached even by phone. Mark was a friendly guy who was always positive.

After one month, it was time to return home and find where things had been left off with Charles. Charles's energy was hovering above Mary's house. Once she returned, Mary could feel the dark energy consume the house. It was time for cleaning. Charles always felt he had the upper hand with Mary, but he never really hurt her to the point of suffocation. At times, the idea crossed his mind but he could not do that to her. He did not treat her as he treated the others. He swore vengeance to all who did not go his way and he wanted to destroy Mary's way of life. He wanted to destroy the happiness, joy and abundance that she so rightly deserved. Charles wanted that energy for many reasons but he was not permitted to have it. Charles brought destruction to Mary's Life and all Mary could think about was fleeing. Mary still had not found the answer to her life's mystery. It appeared that she had not found it in far off lands or with any-one she had spoken to thus far.

Charles decided to go to Nevada where there were certain holes in the ground that pointed to darkness. He arranged to meet with the others for one reason or another, met with him to heal wounds that were of a dark nature. One hole, called, "The Blue Hole," was a deep hole that reached to dark passages in the dark forbidden zone. This hole reached the darkness that was connected to a grid throughout the United States. When anyone who was of a dark nature, felt they needed to resurge their evilness, all they did was drop a line down this hole and recited a few words to connect. The other hole was called, "The Ranch Hole." It was on a ranch that few knew its whereabouts. This hole was used for special purposes when favors of the dark needed to be granted. This hole, in theory, connected with the dark one, or so they say. Sheila informed Mary of these things since she could see all. Charles met with a group he felt he could control. Through this small group of undesirables, he connected his energy in hopes of freeing himself from his heart troubles. Oh, how Charles tried to sift the energy from those around him, but nothing worked. He connected to the energy of these holes but nothing transpired. Charles began to worry with much apprehension and anxiety. After three weeks of chanting and much sorcery performed Charles returned without being healed. His energy began to subside and retreat. His hopes were dashed. His evilness didn't change and he never gave up and he never removed himself from the feelings he had for Mary. If anything were to happen to him, Charles wanted to know that he was successful with not letting Mary meet her soul mate.

In this fashion, the never-ending saga would continue in the next life when Charles, under a different name, would pursue Mary.

This plot would have been successful if it weren't for Mary understanding the workings of Charles' mind. She, too, kept a routine check on this scrupulous character who would not let go. Perhaps, all that was needed was for Mary to reach a certain vibration in order to emanate the light well hidden by Charles. That spiritual light needed to come out. The shadow side had been too dark and grim. The imbalance was far too evident, but no one knew how to fix Mary's consistent, needed daily balance. Someone had to help her, but who? As we look for the answer, and pray for the answer to be given, patience wears thin and we wonder if it will come at all. And then it appears. Mary searched healers online and found a prodigy, the answer to her dreams. She was directed to him and he found the cure. As he spoke, she immediately healed. Each malady was healed as she had asked. It was like magic and it truly was a miracle. After four years of suffering and ridicule, Mary reached her freedom. Her angels and guides watched over her with all those who helped her persevere and pursue the righteous freedom, she so rightly deserved. Mary's crime was meeting the big bad wolf in sheep's clothing. The devil behind the angel of misguided direction who changed people's lives with a stroke of his hands and moved with the silent sting of a cobra. Why give this insane abomination any energy at all? Whenever you speak the name of someone, that vibration can be heard if tapped into by others.

Mary prayed every day and knew that the Supreme Being answered prayers without hesitancy. Sometimes, the answer comes soon and sometimes it comes later. Mary learned the lesson and learned to listen to that small voice. Mary's

persistence won over the never-ending negative being, and
Mary knew this. We take so much for granted, but in Mary's
case, freedom of the soul was an important lesson that she
needed not be reminded of. Those who are kind and seek to
help others become an easy target for those who want to take
advantage. Have we forgotten that kindness is not a
weakness? Just maybe, it would take only one person to make
him change. Sometimes, we do not know how we are used to
fulfill a purpose. Mary was just happy to be free and alive.

Although she needed to distinguish the trail of negativity
that Charles left, Mary knew she was finally free. If we obtain
enlightenment in this life, we can say that our soul is free and
may choose never to come back to earth. If Mary
orchestrated this lesson prior to her birth, only to learn a
lesson from, surely she learned this lesson. This lesson never
needs to be repeated. Trauma and confusion was left in the
wake of the lesson she would never forget. The prodigy that
helped Mary told her that seven past lives with Charles had
been extinguished. He had repeated most of these lives with
Mary in this lifetime and all but one remained. The life of
Atlantis was brought back to this lifetime. Charles had
destroyed Mary and her soul mate in a fiendish plot with
crystals. He, Mary and her soul mate all perished in the blink
of an eye. There would be no more blinking in this lifetime
when all was out in the open. Thank the Supreme Being that
the prodigy found the key to her freedom, she was forever
grateful. Mary could have been locked in a Rubik Cube that
might never have been solved. Her whole life began to
transform in front of her eyes. Her light side integrated and
overshadowed her darkness. Never would she be inclined to

lean towards her vices and her heavenly peace was returned intact and unharmed. Every moment is precious and Mary would never take anything for granted, especially her freedom to be herself. Mary was then sent an angel Mary alone was responsible for. Few are asked to change their life, but this is what she was asked to do. If she did not change her life, the angel suffered by her choices. This angel would remove obstacles in her life and Mary had to believe that this would happen. Mary knew that she had to overcome this fear and move on. To change her ways and to change her habits was not an easy feat. Being responsible for an angel was a heavy responsibility, but Mary was up to that mission. Mary never let anyone know it but she found that she had to commit to this angel because who would disobey an angel?

It took Mary some time to recover her health. For those who loved Mary, they saw a new Mary they had not seen before. The light burned brightly in her soul off a burning brightness not seen before. All were amazed at how her brightness surroundeed Mary. There were those who heard of Mary's miracle and came to see it for themselves.

Charles had been consumed with hatred and jealousy that rose like flames in a furnace that never ceased. He felt so unhappy and miserable to the point of retaliation. The wall of light would not let him move forward or backward. He was a statue of motionless rhythm. His assistant and those who helped him fell back with shock and bewilderment as that transpired. They would never touch Mary again. No matter how they tried, no one could penetrate the light that was blinding to the eye. Charles tried his bat medicine to become small as a tiny bat and pierce a hole in Mary's aura. However, this too, did not work. He tried to encircle her with darkness that loomed like the soot of bonfire, but that did not work either. One by one, Charles tried many things to defeat Mary. But nothing worked. The fist of consternation beat down the Belief of his righteousness and indignation. "How could this happen?" He tried everything and this time it did not work. Charles would not look into the mirror. The mirror in his room reflected an ugly villain with an ugly frame of bones that showed horror and disproportionate balance. He finally looked and saw the monster that he had become. This monster appeared as the monster he had seen as a child. He had become what he feared. Poor Charles finally felt some remorse For what he had done to others. The cry for much needed love was never answered. Those cries of suffering that were endured by those Charles had touched were never answered either.

Mary put an advertisement in the paper hoping to find all who had been touched by Charles. All came forward with much enthusiasm to connect to her. Upon their meeting, all discussed what they had endured. Spoken words left Mary in awe and disbelief. She could not fathom how they all kept this force within them without any outlet. Their energies had been stripped of all decency and became fluid that was not their own. Their light became bright and unencumbered by darkness. Once Mary was able to defeat Charles, it would not be hard for her to find her soul mate.

The constant yearning that could not be dismissed kept Mary awake at night. What was her soul mate doing, could he hear her when she cried out for him at night? The thoughts about someone you love are ever perplexing, especially when you know they can be with someone else. Charles continued his madness with jealousy and would not allow anyone to come between Mary and himself. Oh, how Mary would wish that Charles fell into a hole deep enough to go to the core of the earth and never come out. Mary had to defend herself and could not always think about her soul mate, as it would sadden Her more to think that he could be with someone other than her. Charles continued to keep contained in his mind control games each day and under close watch. He did not want Mary and her soul mate to meet under any circumstances.

We all vibrate at a certain vibration. Mary's vibration was well imprinted and shared amongst Charles's cronies. Charles had paid two women to track Mary. They were a unified bunch. Charles could not do this on his own; he was not omnipresent. Mary, in turn, had to cloak herself so that Charles would never know where she went. This was not an easy feat, as few knew how to cloak.

Cloaking took time and time was what Mary did not have, especially when under attack each day. Mary wondered why she was not taught how to cloak amongst her healer friends. It appeared to her as an essential part of life that was omitted and left her vulnerable. Not everyone is exposed to the dark side of life. Many carry on without hindrances. Those who have hardships are the ones that grow. Mary was determined to escape the clutches of Charles and not live in hiding or fear. Damned the torpedoes, Mary was not going to sit down and be intimidated by an advisory with a mythical-God Complex and played with lives as though it were a game. The wheel of fortune is not to be tampered with. For every spin backwards, Mary was determined to march forward. She was entitled to live her life unhampered, aren't we all? Those slimy and creepy cronies of Charles fought for something they truly did not understand. Their outstretched hands looked to be paid with money, as though gold doubloons would fall through a sieve into their hands for their dastardly deeds. Their habits of scurrying along when they were called, left dusts of dismay and death, leaving nothing to the imagination. "Get along little doggies. And doggies be gone for good." In their minds, they fought for a cause that Charles had implemented. Only Charles knew that cause, they only obeyed.

Mary one day came across a prodigy in his own right that could see things as psychic Edgar Casey had. His name was Peter and through him, many answers were given. Nothing was left unturned or unquestioned with Peter. He was kind and much in demand. He knew how to find the problem and root it out. Peter could tell you in a matter of seconds how to solve the ailment and then go on to the next without hesitation. Mary's main concern was how to close doors in the shadow side that Charles was getting into. Peter stated, "How to close a shadow door is by envisioning a door in meditation. Command negative draining energy out of it. Mentally see yourself painting over the door with bright white paint and command it to stay closed. This may have to be done on a daily basis for at least three days and repeated as necessary." Mary through this was fantastic and it was music to her ears. Finally, she had found someone who knew of such things and could tell her a plan of action. Peter was precise as an X-acto knife and did not waste any time getting there. He was intuitive and helpful in all facets of Mary's life, and he was going to put an end to all of Mary's adversaries who brought her pain and heartache. No one was ever going to hurt Mary again and Peter would see to that.

His confidence in Mary was never defeated or allowed to die. She believed in herself and knew that no one was to hurt her soul, no matter what Charles or any other was doing to her. That confidence lay in knowing that no one but the Supreme Being has the right to destroy you as a person or take away who you are. They have no right; they have no justice. We are all children of the Supreme Being, even the evil ones are of the Divine Plan. Let not your confidence ever be shaken. Even when all hope is dashed, there is still the thought of hope. And all thoughts have power. Mind control done by Charles could be pushed aside by knowing thy self and keeping what is true to you alone. When your connection is broken from the Divine, there is hope of reconnection. When your connection to your self is broken, there is always hope to get your true self back. And when the connection to finding the love of your life is forgotten, there is always hope that you will find them. All vices that are pitted against you or that you find is too alluring, you can always have the strength to say no. Charles tried all of these and yet Mary continued onward without hesitation. She never gave up and she never stopped hoping. Was it Peter that finally gave her hope, or was the Supreme Being working with Peter to finally let Mary know that it was time to answer her prayer and for God to know that Mary had passed her trials and tribulations? Mary passed her tests. Many of Mary's friends stated that her karma at this time had been complete and it was time for Peter to appear. But Mary knew different. This was much more than karma, it was a test of faith. Just how much could Mary endure depended on her faith and her ability to believe in herself. That was all there was. Surely, the Supreme Being would have allowed the one hundred demons to consume her and at times the physical suffering that she endured by Charles was too much to Bear. Praying everyday and getting closer to the Supreme Being saved her life and saved her soul. So, maybe Charles did serve a purpose maybe Charles fit into the scheme of Things with the contract Mary had written prior to coming into this world. Only the Supreme Being truly knew that answer. One thing for sure, Mary was truly appreciative of life and all that it had to offer. She trusted the higher power and wherever her destiny sent her.

Finding the soul mate became easy once Charles subsided. Mary's soul mate had come to the understanding that Charles had orchestrated the one woman who had been flattering his ego. His mind control on the woman contributed to the soul mate's subconscious. He soon awakened from a stupor to realize that all the woman wanted was his money. Never did Charles stop his evil ways, they just weakened. His Energy on others eventually and slowly subsided. The woman who was trying to flatter Mary's soul mate had her own agenda. She had gone to others to perform sorcery and obtain what she wanted, clever soul. This woman soon met her fate when she was confronted with a wall of distress that would not permit her to go beyond her scope. All her friends had tried, fell with disappointment and sorrow. Once this occurred, she fell with anger and despair. Mary's soul mate was thankful to the awakening and the heartache that he may have known. When dark forces fell upon the soul mate, his sadness and confusion laid a heavy hand. Mary tried to send messages to him and tried to let him know that she was waiting for him and that there was hope. These forces became quite manipulative and debilitating. When we love someone so deeply, we know in our hearts that this will not last forever. Mary would not stop until all was overcome. That bully Charles, who had to control all in his environment and be a God in his own right! Pull the abomination down, until it is no more and never to be again! Much is to be discovered about Asperger's Syndrome and in the case of Charles, what can be harnessed and discarded for the good of mankind. Peter, the healer, was the key to Mary's freedom. Once through the door, Peter was able to turn circumstances around that were unbelievable to Mary. Peter was much more than a prodigy, he was a walking miracle to many and a new beginning for Mary and her soul mate.

Peter once remarked, "In the waters off the southwest coast of Africa, the small fish known as the bearded goby has always preyed upon the jellyfish, until recently. Now this formerly mild-mannered species, whose diet used to consist of Phytoplankton, has overthrown the ancient status quo. It is Feasting on the jellyfish that once feasted on it. Scientists aren't sure why. I foresee a metaphorically comparable development in your life. How it will play out exactly, I'm not sure. Maybe, you'll gain an advantage over someone or something that has always had an advantage over you. Maybe, you will become the top dog in a place where you've been the underdog. Or maybe, you'll begin drawing energy from a source that has in the past sucked your energy." Mary just listened as Peter rhetorically gave this example. But Mary knew victory was at hand and no more did fear over take her, and no more would she question much in her life.

The signs to look for when people are exhibiting strange behaviors are many as Peter mentioned. The stance of someone demonstrates much about what they want to not convey. Sometimes, people exhibit odd behavior and do not show their true motives. Once entering your house, they act suspiciously and do not remark about anything until you do. Although, someone may have an impediment that does not necessarily mean something bad, again that little voice should let you know that there is something wrong. Peter went on to say that each day when we wake up, we need to ask to be protected by the white light and make a motion with our hands and arms to circle our whole body. In this way, we are cleared of any negative energies that encircle us. If you find yourself thinking about someone who is bothering you, ask yourself, are these my thoughts or someone else's? In Mary's case, someone was sending her energies that were not her own. So, Mary quickly changed her thoughts about that person. When you're thinking about someone, you bring them closer to you. Maybe, someone is sending you unhappy or depressing thoughts or do not have your best interests at heart. In this way, it is important to pray and keep your thoughts lighthearted, concerning love and laughter. Some people think of angels, deities or holy ones. Mary pictured Jesus in her mind and then all thoughts of Charles disappeared. Our intent is focus plus faith. Visualization is great when we can utilize this action. As in the case of Charles and Mary, Mary focused on titanium steel surrounding her because this was the only material in the spiritual realm that kept Charles out. Charles once told Mary That he could not visualize due to his Asperger's Syndrome. Mary was at an advantage due to the fact she could do this quite well. She envisioned herself with mirrors all around her each day, reflecting out, and then she built walls of brick at a certain width and depth. On rare occasions, she would send her angels and tell the angels to take Charles where he needed to go. This happened only when Charles was bothering Mary all the time. His fixation on her kept her on her toes until she was nudged to do something about it, which was often. Mary could also distinguish his smell. Energies have smells and once these energies become regular, a defense mechanism kicks in and a person's defense combat's their adversary's. Mary also knew someone who could clone her on occasion. Mary was assured that after one hundred Mary's, it would be difficult for Charles to find the real Mary. Unfortunately, Mary could not locate her friend who did it the first two times. Nevertheless, Mary had fun doing this as it confused Charles so. Mary had difficulty allowing others do her work for her. At times, it is good to have someone to pray for you. In unison, prayer becomes strength and nervousness is replaced by calm. It is our emotions that Charles was feeding off and our emotions are our private response to our essence. It is not a matter of expressing ourselves, it is important to be in the company of those we trust before expressing our true selves. Unless the feeling of trust is felt, we need not express all our emotions out in the open due to others taking that energy. This is an important Lesson that we need to learn because there are those that feed off your emotions and this

can easily be a problem when all are not on the same
wavelength as you. By the second week of meeting someone,
usually you can tell what they are all about. Mary was able to
understand Charles in that first week, yet Mary did not listen
nor adhere to that small still voice. She regretted having felt
sorry for Charles even though he had Asperger's Syndrome.
Guarding your wellbeing is paramount in all that you say and
do. We forget ourselves and think of ourselves last. This is
our first and last mistake and in Mary's case, Charles was
counting on it. Thus, Mary became easy prey in his eyes. In
this respect, Charles never hurt Mary to the fullest because he
felt she could not defend herself fully. Maybe this was a good
thing. Nevertheless, Mary was always trying this or that to
keep Charles and his cronies out. This was not easy since
Charles was taught by the best of them, his mother and all
those that knew him, at an early age. Once anyone came to
understand what was happening to her, no one knew if she
suffered from a malady that needed to be seen by a doctor or
some energy needed to be lifted from her. Although all the
angels and Ascended Masters were behind her, finding a
solution was part of the battle.

Chapter 11

COMPLAINING ABOUT WHAT is happening to you does no good because most people do not want to talk about the dark. Knowing what you need to do to help yourself is half of the battle. Peter made sure that all was understood by Mary and that Mary would adhere to certain self defense rules so that She would never be defenseless. It is through time that all wounds are healed. Mary found time to forgive Charles for what he did and at times, it was quite difficult. Everyone, in their own time, needs to forgive the person who has done them wrong. This is not only releases their wrongdoings, but also releases them from constantly thinking about it.

"For if ye forgive men their trespasses, your heavenly Father will also forgive you: But if ye forgive not men their trespasses neither will your Father forgive your trespasses." Mathew 6:14

Mary kept this passage in her mind since she heard Charles's voice trying to control her thoughts. Charles took her life, but Mary knew that she would survive and she knew in the end that she would be victorious. Charles fed off her darkness, her shadow side and that was all he could ever reach. Once all the energy was used, and then the door would be forever closed. No matter how hard Charles tried to open that door, it was forever sealed. Thieves and murderers walk in darkness, and Mary walked in the light. She was the light and beacon to things Charles did not understand and, sadly, would never know.

Prior to meeting Richard, Mary's soul mate, Mary had an idea of calling a bookstore that Richard attended regularly. She decided to call for a man named Richard. Mary saw his name in her dreams and decided to call her soul mate as such. To her disappointment, he did not come to the phone when his name was announced. Charles kept one step ahead of Mary by making sure that her soul mate had other women as distractions. Charles would circle the area of the soul mate with his remote viewing capacities and then use mind control on a woman nearby to distract Richard by appealing to his male gaze. That woman did not love Mary's soul mate at all, but kept Richard from looking for Mary.

Although, the woman was attached to Mary's soul mate's subconscious, he found that he was slipping under an uncontrollable negative influence. All the good and spiritual foundation of Mary's soul mate was at a crossroad, and that crossroad was between the outer realm of his shadow and that of the light. Mary's soul mate did not know that Charles was feeding on his mind on a daily basis with negative and evil thoughts. Each day Charles would blend his thoughts with Mary's soul mate's thoughts until Richard began to feel that these thoughts were his own. Mary would cry in horror of such things happening. She could not save her soul mate but only pray and try to find him to shake him off this scrupulous character, Charles. That scrupulous character shifted to other personalities with each appearance when it suited him. His disguise kept him fooling most who followed his trail of deceit. Charles continued to laugh to himself, but this time he felt he had fulfilled a vendetta from another lifetime. Charles deep down loved Mary in some odd strange way. Mary asked, "Why would someone want to do these things?" The evil way of Charles would fit that profile. Charles with malice and discontent of never knowing the meaning of love and never loving anyone, found this whole situation quite amusing. He continued to want Mary for himself and if he could not have her, no one would. Charles would also whisper to Richard that he would never find Mary, so stop looking! Although, at first, Richard did not agree with this and pushed Charles's suggestions out of his mind. Over time, it became difficult for him to convince himself that Mary was waiting patiently. Charles was eager to push all thoughts of Mary completely out of Richard's mind. Oh, the depths of darkness can swirl around the body and pull anyone down, down until they are swimming in a pool of everlasting nothingness and a vice that is hard to crawl out from. The darkness was too encompassing for Mary's soul mate to overcome. The darkness of Charles would not let him be free.

Mary continued her search to find, win, and rescue Richard from this entwined vine of darkness even if that meant battling the woman who had wrapped her claws into her soul mate and would not let go.

Mary fought this energy with all her might and her soul mate tried with much constant ambivalence. Charles laughed to himself when Richard would reach for higher guidance only to be shot down with a strong negative energy. That ugly soul!

Charles felt that he needed to teach Mary and Richard a thing or two. No one was going to take his Mary away from him, even if they were meant to be together. "Just let God put them together after I get through with them!" he muttered to himself. He never got that chance. Charles had lost that battle.

Richard was pitted against his fears that Charles knew so well. He had all temptations thrown at him to disrupt Mary's meeting him. What Charles could never understand was the meaning of love and how as hard as he tried to break the relationship, nothing would happen as a result. This was an enigma for Charles and nothing but his mother's love exemplified his understanding partially. Love was an emotion that Charles knew nothing about. What Charles could not feel was the love that Mary carried with her for so long.

Mary never saw Charles again after the door was shut. He was never allowed near her and she never thought of him. Her fear became null with all that she closed. Moreover, whoever hurt or bothered Mary would suffer unspeakable woe condemning their souls to unimaginable tragedies. Mary would walk with everlasting love and harmony few experience in this world. Mary found her soul mate and together their love was of the purest form. And many looked upon them with envy. They were a handsome couple with enduring trust and love for each other. Mary's soul mate was of royal blood. They both took life with much gusto and much weaving between the fabrics of life. This made him quite heroic and very much a free spirit in Mary's eyes. They met at a festival when both took each other by surprise. They knew instantly that they were made for each other. The pangs of love were too much to bear at first, for both realized that time was unkind to them and that Charles , that sinister devil, made it so.

Her soul mate's name was Richard and they instantly acquainted themselves with one another and were soon finishing each other's sentences. From this day forward, they decided to put the past behind them and start each day as though they had just met. The Supreme Being loves those who head out the adventure of love, and always lets these people wander between clouds, without the risk of falling and getting hurt. No one could come between them. Not even Charles! Their love was far too strong for even Charles's dark forces to break them apart. Bu oh, how he tried!

Charles had a door closed that was never to open. His fists shook with such anger and rage, not to speak of, revenge. To this day, no one knew what happened to Charles. His cronies were gone. Even his cronies did not know where Charles had slithered away to. They shook their heads in disbelief and shock at Charles's abandonment. Some saw Charles leaving town with his old car and waving goodbye to all that he had known.

Many a story followed Charles as he left that day. One man told a story he had heard about Charles from another months earlier. As Charles was leaving all behind, he had a flat tire. As he fixed this tire, a sheriff helped him. The sheriff then noticed that Charles was wanted for illegal possession of a firearm and arrested him. Charles waited to go to court for three weeks. He could not wait anymore and hanged himself in his jail cell. His conscious could not take anymore.

Another man, weeks later, stated that Charles's tumor had affected his entire mind and that other tumors had spread throughout his body. Like the friend Charles had seen in the hospital, he too met with a similar fate. Charles could not remember who he was or where he was going. They say he was driven mad! A mad man for whom he had once thought he would never be. He remains in a bed in an old nursing home, a forgotten soul, forgotten with time.

Another man spoke of quite a different matter. He spoke of the group, Aloscha, which had taken Charles and removed his brain. Together with other brains, three to be exact, Charles's brain was put in a cave. There, in the cave, the brains were kept until the earth plunged into darkness. At the time, the group thought they would control all brains and rule over the world. What a frightening thought! When Mary heard these things, she thought this was the most frightening. These evil souls had no remorse and no light. Their secrecy was of grave ignorance of life. Mary did not want to hear anymore. The mere thought of this kept her wondering for quite some time.

The least bizarre story of all was that a tumor had grown so large in Charles's head that he died of heart complications.

If only he was that lucky! Mary believed this ending to keep her mind at peace. No marker was ever found, nor any urn ever reported. Nevertheless, Mary knew that Charles was not on earth.

"Get along little doggie, get along." Charles met his dear mother on the other side, and once again, they were together and found their connection, the connection not of the divine, but of darkness and evilness that remained bound. When Charles left this plane, earth, all those he had affected and made to suffer was lifted and returned to their ways of happiness and joy. They, too, started a new life after learning many lessons and appreciated this second chance at life.

But a few years later, a friend thought he had caught the glimpse of someone who resembled Charles. Ah, but that couldn't be him, could it?

Epilogue

ALTHOUGH THE BATTLE had ceased, in Charles's mind he would use every means to continue. There was no more energy left in his frail body but he worked through the energies of others to regain his strength. They were a vehicle to house him until he took their energy to execute his dastardly deeds. When Kathleen, his hidden accomplice, and all his cronies pulled away, they could not keep up to his new idea of onslaught. Besides, they had already accrued heavy karma helping Charles, and they wanted no more. Charles was left defenseless. However, there was always tomorrow to find new alliances. This was all about jealousy and bullying. He kept repeating to himself, "I never lose." His insanity reckoned with his subconscious. The mighty engine of evil came to a halt. He was all alone except for his dear mother who kept vigilant watch over him from the other side, and every once in awhile appeared to remind him who was really in control.

www.ingramcontent.com/pod-product-compliance
Lightning Source LLC
Chambersburg PA
CBHW050308260626
47156CB00005B/1715